across

a hundred

mountains

across
a hundred
mountains

a novel

REYNA GRANDE

ATRIA BOOKS

New York London Toronto Sydney

ATRIA BOOKS
1230 Avenue of the Americas
New York, NY 10020

Library of Congress Cataloging-in-Publication Data

Grande, Reyna.
   Across a hundred mountains : a novel / Reyna Grande.— 1st Atria Books hardcover ed.
     p. cm.
    1. Immigrants—Fiction. 2. Emigration and immigration—Fiction. 3. Southwestern States—Fiction. 4. Mexico, North—Fiction. I. Title.

PS3607.R3627A63 2006
813'.6—dc22

                     2005057125

ISBN-13: 978-0-7432-6957-5
ISBN-10:   0-7432-6957-8

First Atria Books hardcover edition June 2006

10 9 8 7 6 5 4 3 2 1

ATRIA BOOKS is a trademark of Simon & Schuster, Inc.

Manufactured in the United States of America

For information about special discounts for bulk purchases, please contact Simon & Schuster Special Sales at 1-800-456-6798 or business@simonandschuster.com.

to my son, Nathaniel,

and to those who have

perished trying to get

to El Otro Lado

across

a hundred

mountains

adelina

"That's your father's grave," the old man repeated, in a voice that was barely audible. He'd been silent most of the crossing. When he had to speak at all, he did so softly, as if this place was as holy as church.

The U.S. border.

Adelina looked at the large pile of rocks he was pointing to. The old man had to be mistaken. Her father wasn't under there. He couldn't be.

She wiped the sweat from her forehead with the back of her hand. Then she used her hand as a shield to cover her eyes from the glare of the sun. She took a few steps forward until she was in the shadow of a boulder towering above them and the pile of rocks.

Could her father really be buried there?

She gulped. Her mouth was dry, and swallowing made her throat ache, as if she were swallowing a prickly pear, spines and all. She felt tears burning her eyes and quickly rubbed them dry.

"It's not too late to turn around and go back," the old man said. "Maybe it would be best."

Adelina took a deep breath, then turned to look at the sea of shrub and cactus stretching out around her. The terrain seemed to never end. It had taken almost all day to get here. They hadn't been caught by the immigration patrol this time.

She looked back at the old man. He must have been a good coyote back in the day when he was young and agile. Even now, with sixty years on his back, a bad eye, and a lame knee, he'd managed to get her past the ever-watching eyes of la migra on their second attempt.

"We can turn around now," the old man said again. "You've seen his grave, let that be enough."

Adelina shook her head and began to walk down to the pile. "I didn't come to see a grave," she said as she took off her backpack. "I came to find my father, and I will take him with me, even if I have to carry his bones on my back."

The old man looked at her with surprise. Adelina didn't look at his good brown eye. Instead, she looked at his left eye, the one with the blue film over it. She had discovered that this was the only way she could make the old man look away. The old man looked back at the rocks and said nothing.

Yet Adelina knew what he was thinking. She had lied to him. She had not told him she was planning to dig up the body and, if it really was her father, take him back with her. He would not have brought her here had she told him this.

She bent down and began to remove the rocks one by one. So many rocks on top of him. So much weight to support. Maybe once the rocks were gone, maybe once he was free, she, too, would be free.

"It may not even be him," the old man said as he grabbed her wrist to stop her from removing any more rocks.

"I have to know," Adelina said. "For nineteen years I have not known what happened to my father. You have no idea what it's like to live like that—not to know. Hoy sabré la verdad." She yanked her arm and continued removing the rocks. The old man walked away from her.

She tried to hurry. One by one the rocks were lifted. Some rocks rolled down and hit her knees. Her fingers began to hurt from being scraped. There was still a possibility the old man was right. Maybe it wasn't her father. But which would be worse, that it was her father or that it wasn't?

Nineteen years not knowing. Too many years thinking he had abandoned them.

"Look!" the old man said.

Adelina turned around and saw a cloud of dust rising in the distance.

"La migra," the old man said. "We must hide."

Adelina turned back to the rocks and in desperation began throwing them against the boulder. The sound echoed against the settled dust. She had to know who was buried there. She had to see for herself if it really was her father.

"What are you doing? Hide!" The old man quickly made his way to a crevice in the boulder. But Adelina kept throwing off the rocks and didn't move from where she was.

"Let them come," she said. "Let la migra find us. Maybe they can help us take this man's bones back—" She gasped at the sight of a small metal cross. She quickly lifted more rocks and then covered her mouth with her hand to stifle a cry. She looked at the old man, at his bad eye, but this time the old man didn't look away.

"It's a white rosary with heart-shaped beads, yes?" he asked.

Adelina nodded, looking down at the rusted metal cross, at the white beads, at the bones that had once been a hand.

The old man hadn't lied.

"He was clutching the rosary so tightly when I found him dead, right there where he is now," the old man said. "It's as if he had been praying right until his death. Praying for a miracle, perhaps."

"That son-of-a-bitch coyote just left him here to die!" Adelina said.

"Your father was bitten by a snake. The coyote probably left him here thinking la migra would find him. Look, here they come now."

Adelina turned around and saw a white vehicle approaching. La migra was here.

But they were nineteen years too late to save her father.

juana

Mexico

Juana looked at her mother standing in the doorway. Amá was trying to see through the watery veil and down the road, hoping Apá would appear. She'd been there for over an hour as the rain filled the puddles outside. Juana rocked the hammock back and forth inside the shack, humming a song to her baby sister, Anita, who would not fall asleep. It was as if Anita was also waiting for Apá to come home.

Darkness fell and the rain continued. Juana lay in her cot, wondering where Apá was. He was a campesino, and he worked in the fields planting and harvesting crops on the other side of the river. She knew that once in a while he would be delayed if someone got hurt with a machete, or bitten by a snake. Could something have happened to her father? If so, why wasn't anyone coming to tell them?

Amá sighed as she wrapped her rebozo tight around her. Her dress was wet, her legs were speckled with mud, but still she stood, exposed to the elements, refusing to warm herself inside the shack and eat a bowl of beans.

"Tu padre no llega," she said to Juana as she gave one more glance up the road, before she finally came inside. She headed straight to the altar in the corner where many statues of saints were glowing from the light of the candles. She took her rosary out from her brassiere and gently caressed the shiny, black beads.

"Maybe he can't cross the river," Juana said, joining her mother at the altar. She knew that sometimes when it rained hard, the river swelled, making it impossible for anyone to cross. Sometimes it swelled so much the water would overflow, creeping into the shacks like un ladrón, a thief.

Amá nodded, then knelt on the dirt floor and made the sign of the cross. Juana watched the flame of the candle flickering on La Virgen de Guadalupe's brown face and dedicated all her prayers to her. Then she picked up her rosary and kissed the metal cross hanging from it. Apá gave her this rosary the day of her first communion, a year and a half ago, on her tenth birthday.

"Ave María Purísima," Amá said.

"Sin pecado concevida," Juana added. Their voices filled the shack and lulled Anita to sleep. As they prayed, Juana was glad their voices drowned out the unforgiving rain beating on their tar-soaked cardboard roof.

The rain didn't want to be silenced by their prayers. Thunder shook the walls, making the bamboo sticks rattle like wet bones. Juana said her prayers louder, just in case La Virgencita couldn't properly hear her. After a while her throat ached, and still, Apá did not come.

Her prayers became softer and softer, until they were

merely whispers, until she only echoed every other word her mother said. Then, finally, it was only her mother praying.

Juana's eyes wanted to close. She'd been kneeling for so long she could no longer feel her bony knees. But she couldn't leave Amá alone to wait for her father. The image of La Virgen blurred in front of her. Her body swayed to one side. Her rosary fell to the dirt floor.

"Go to bed, Juana," her mother said in a raspy voice. "You've done your part, my daughter."

Juana shook her head and opened her mouth to say another prayer, but she could no longer think of any.

"Go to sleep. I'll wake you when Apá comes home." Amá made the sign of the cross in front of Juana and tried to help her get up. Juana couldn't stand up, so instead, she crawled all the way to her cot, being careful not to spill any of the pots Amá had placed around the shack to catch the rainwater leaking through the roof.

Juana was wet all over when she woke up. For a brief moment, she felt embarrassed, thinking she had peed her bed. Her mother stood beside the cot, holding a candle. Even in the dim candlelight Juana could see the shack flooded with water.

"The river has flooded," Amá said. "We must get on the table." She was cradling Anita in one arm. Juana noticed that Amá's wet dress clung to her, as if afraid.

Amá turned around and waded to the small dining table. Juana's body trembled as she lowered her legs into the cold water. The water reached to her waist. She guided herself by the flame of the candle her mother held and made her way to the table, pushing plastic cups, clothes, pieces of cardboard, soggy tortillas, flowers, and candlesticks out of the way. She glanced in the direction where the altar should have been, but all she saw was water.

Juana got on top of the table and sat next to her mother. Both tucked their feet underneath their legs.

"It's the river that doesn't let Miguel come home," Amá said. Juana nodded. She wondered if Apá knew the shack had flooded. She hoped that soon he would try to cross the river to come for them and take them to town, to her godmother's house. There they would be warm and dry.

Juana leaned against her mother and listened to Anita's sucking sounds as she nursed from Amá's large, round breast.

"Don't worry, mi'ja," Amá said. "Your father will come for us soon. Tomorrow the rain will stop, and the river waters will go back down."

The rain continued, and the river waters did not recede. By now their bodies shivered and their stomachs growled, but they were helpless to do anything about it. Only Anita was warm inside her mother's rebozo. And only her stomach was soothed by her mother's milk. Juana clutched her stomach tight and tried not to think about how hungry or cold she was, or how heavy her eyelids felt. She only thought about Apá. Soon, he would come for them. Soon, they would be at her madrina's house, drinking a cup of hot chocolate, all of them together.

A few hours after daylight, there was still no sign of Apá. Amá waded through the water and yanked the door open. The sky was still heavy with clouds, and the rain was now falling in a drizzle.

"I'll go look for help," Amá said. She walked back to Juana and handed her the baby.

"But Amá—"

"I must try to make it to Don Agustín's house farther down the river. They have a boat. Maybe they can row us to the other side."

Juana grabbed her sister and held her tight. The baby let out a cry and opened her arms to her mother.

Amá shook her head. "Stay with your sister, Anita. Mami will come back soon."

Juana lowered her head as Amá made the sign of the cross and blessed her.

Amá took off her shawl and placed it over Anita. "I won't be long. Take good care of your sister, Juana. Hold her tight and don't let go of her."

"I won't, Amá," Juana said as she tightened her hold on Anita. She leaned against the wall and sat very still on top of the table. Amá looked at them one more time and then struggled back to the door, splashing the muddy water as she left.

Juana watched the ripples her mother had made get smaller and smaller. Soon, the water settled down again. It was so still, as if Amá had never walked through it.

". . . Dios te salve María, llena eres de gracia, bendita eres entre todas las mujeres y bendito es el fruto de tu vientre, Jesús. Amén." Juana wet her lips with her tongue. Her throat was dry, but she kept praying because every time she paused she could hear the rain pouring down again. Why couldn't it stop raining?

Anita stirred awake once more and began to make funny sucking noises. She pressed closer to Juana, searching for her mother's breasts.

"There, there, Anita, go back to sleep." Juana rocked the baby up and down. Anita wailed and waved her fists in the air. "Go to sleep, Anita, go to sleep."

The baby's cries cut straight through Juana's ears, leaving them ringing. Juana began to pray once more, hoping the sound of her voice would make her sister go to sleep. But Anita cried and cried. Juana put her finger inside Anita's mouth. Anita latched on to it quickly and immediately began sucking on it. Juana smiled at the tingling she felt on the tip of her finger. But too soon, Anita pushed the finger away and let out another loud scream.

"Please come soon, Apá," Juana said over and over again. Her eyelids began to close. She tried to grab some water to splash on her face, but she couldn't reach it. She held Anita tight as she pushed herself closer to the edge of the table. Her hand slipped from under her and she almost fell.

After what seemed an eternity, Anita finally fell asleep sucking on her tiny fist. The sound of the rain falling on the roof began to penetrate Juana's sleepy mind. It was still raining. Her parents still hadn't come.

Juana's body trembled, her stomach had begun to eat itself, and it seemed her eyelids were tied to rocks. She forced her left eye open with one hand while she held her sister with the other. The right eye closed, demanding sleep. Juana wondered if it was possible to let her right eye sleep, while the left eye kept guard.

"I must not fall asleep," she told herself. "I must not fall asleep, I must not . . ."

adelina

Adelina listened to the sounds inside the dark airplane. All around her people were snoring. Even the man sitting next to her was leaning back on his seat, his eyes closed, his chest rising and falling to the rhythm of his snores. The sound was annoying, but Adelina was not annoyed. She tried to imagine that the snores were coming from her, that it was she who was enjoying a good sleep.

Sleep.

Even thinking about that word hurt.

The man next to her leaned against Adelina and loudly snored in her ear. She didn't push him off. The sound reminded her of her father. There was once a time when he had enjoyed a good sleep like this.

She looked down at the wooden box on her lap and pressed it against her. Her father's ashes. Her redemption. Perhaps after she delivered the ashes to her dying mother there would be no more demons to haunt her, and she would be able to lower her head on a pillow and sleep.

Finally sleep.

juana

"Juana, wake up, wake up."

Juana opened her eyes. She could barely see her mother leaning over her. It was dark in the shack, and she wondered what time it was.

"Cómo está mi Juanita?"

"Apá!" Juana said. Behind Amá, her father and two other men were standing in the water. Juana lifted her arms to him so he would come and hug her. The shawl on her lap fell down to the water, and that was when Juana realized that something was gone. What had she been holding so tightly right before she fell asleep?

"Juana, where's your sister?" Amá asked.

Juana rubbed her sleepy eyes. Amá grabbed her by the shoulders and shook her.

"Where's Anita, Juana? Answer me!"

"Where's your sister?" Apá asked as he stepped forward. Juana looked down at the water, but it was too hard to see anything in the darkness.

She covered her ears to block out her mother's scream.

Amá dropped to her knees and frantically flapped her arms, splashing the water as she searched. Apá and the other men bent down and did the same. Only Juana did nothing. She pressed her knees against her chest, feeling her heart beating fast, so fast it was making her dizzy.

"My daughter, where's my daughter!" Amá yelled as she blindly moved her arms in a circle. Then Apá pulled something out of the water, and even in the darkness, Juana could see that it was Anita.

"Nooooo!" Amá yelled as she grabbed the baby from Apá. "No, no, no!"

Juana lowered her head and hid her face inside her cupped hands.

adelina

Adelina took out the rusty white rosary she had in her purse. The rosary had not protected her father as he had lain on the ground, dying. How foolish she had once been, thinking that it would.

She thought about the past week, how she had walked around Tijuana, asking every coyote she met if he had seen or helped her father cross the border.

She knew from experience that coyotes kept things to themselves, so she'd offered a reward to anyone who would help her find her father. She'd offered all her savings. The coyotes had been afraid she was an undercover cop and had kept their mouths shut. She had almost given up.

Three days ago, after walking around downtown Tijuana, inquiring about her father, something strange had happened. An old man followed her as she headed back to her hotel. She walked faster, but even though the old man was limping, he still kept up with her.

She stopped at a corner to wait for the red light to change. The old man got close and asked her a surprising question.

"Was your father carrying a white rosary made of heart-shaped beads?"

Adelina turned to look at him. Under the light of the streetlamp she noticed that he had a film over his left eye.

A long time ago, she'd met a man with an eye like that. She could barely remember this, but she knew it was true.

"Well, did your father have a white rosary?"

"Yes, he had a white rosary. Do you know my father? Do you know where he is?"

Adelina clutched the sleeve of the old man's shirt and looked at his blind eye as she waited for him to answer. The old man didn't look at her; he looked at the green light on the other side of the street.

"Your light is green. You must hurry if you want to cross."

"Forget the light," Adelina said. "Answer my question. Do you know where my father is?"

The old man nodded. "Yes, I know where he is."

"Take me to him, please."

Adelina could sense in him the desire to turn around and leave.

But then he said, "Tomorrow. Tomorrow I'll take you to see your father, then you can finally go home."

Go home?

"Where is he?" she asked. "Is he well, at least?"

The old man looked at her briefly, but then he lowered his gaze once again.

"In the middle of the border, at the foot of a boulder, is a large pile of rocks. Your father is buried there."

juana

Juana watched the candles flickering in the darkness. So many candles surrounding such a tiny coffin. Maybe around a large coffin the candles wouldn't have looked so overwhelming, but Anita had only been a baby.

Juana looked through the cloud of incense smoke at her mother and father. They were holding on to each other and praying along with the neighbors and her father's distant relatives. Four years ago, when her other younger sister died from a scorpion sting, Amá and Apá had held on to each other like now, but Juana had been put in between them, so they could share their grief as a family.

She wondered why they hadn't called her to them now. Wasn't she still part of the family?

She turned around and headed to the door.

"A dónde vas, Juana?" Apá's mother, Abuelita Elena, stood in the doorway. She wasn't praying along with the rest of the women, and Juana wondered why she'd even bothered coming.

"Outside," Juana said. Her grandmother looked at her for a moment, shook her head, and then moved aside to let her pass.

Juana walked to the train tracks in front of her godparents' house. She sat on the rail and prayed silently as the rest of the women chanted inside.

In a few more hours, they would make their way to the cemetery to bury Anita. Juana rubbed her eyes dry. Her tears reminded her of rain. Rain reminded her of floods. And floods reminded her of Anita.

"Juana, what are you doing out here all alone?" Apá asked, making his way toward her. He sat next to her on the rail and picked up some pebbles from the ground. He moved them around in his hand.

"I'm listening to the prayers," Juana said.

Apá was silent for a moment, then wrapped his arm around her and said, "Pain takes time to heal, Juana. In time, we will all heal, especially your mother."

"She'll never forgive me, Apá."

"She will. But you must give her time."

"Do you forgive me, Apá?" Juana looked at her father. He kept looking at the pebbles in his hand.

"It was my fault, Juana. I should've worked harder to get us out of there. I should've worked more hours, and little by little I could've built us a better house closer to town."

"But Apá—"

"I should've tried harder to swim across the river to get to you in time. Then this would never have happened."

"But Apá—"

"Hush, Juana. I never want to hear you say it was your fault. Fue mi culpa. Mi única, maldita culpa!" Apá hurled the pebbles to the ground. "Just give your mother time, Juana. She had already suffered the loss of two children. Now she's lost a third."

María died from a scorpion sting because they didn't have enough money for a doctor and the healing woman couldn't save her. Josefina died before leaving her mother's womb. It was as if she had given up on life, even before she was born. One day she loosened her hold and was stillborn at four months.

Only Juana had survived. And now, Juana wished that she hadn't.

Sleep became a stranger to Apá. Juana knew because she was the same way. Every time she closed her eyes, her mind would shake her to wake up. *You mustn't go to sleep, Juana. You mustn't sleep,* it said to her.

She lay in her cot and strained her eyes to see him. The tiny shafts of moonlight that cut through the gaps between the bamboo sticks were too weak to chase away the darkness, so it wasn't easy. She knew he wasn't sleeping because Apá always snored when he slept. Instead, he breathed in and out softly. Sometimes a sigh would escape his lips, sometimes a curse, sometimes the sounds of weeping. She listened and followed his movements around the shack. He walked up and down, like a trapped animal, then he would drop onto a chair and stay there for hours.

At times like these Juana wished she could get up and go to her father, but she was afraid. And she didn't know why.

. . .

On Sunday, as usual, Juana and her parents made their way alongside the river, then turned and headed up a hill to their favorite rock. They came here once in a while to watch the sunset. Amá, Apá, Juana, María, and later Anita. Apá would point to the crops in the distance and tell them how much he'd harvested that day.

"From there to all the way over there," he would say.

When they got to their spot Juana and Amá sat down on the rock and waited for Apá to sit down. He didn't. Instead, he looked at the stalks of corn gently swaying in the breeze.

"How much corn did you harvest today, Apá?" Juana asked.

Apá scratched his head for a moment, looking down at the tiny colorful houses in the distance. He didn't answer her, and Juana knew he hadn't heard her. She looked at her mother sitting on the rock next to her. Amá was looking down at her hands as if she didn't know what to do with them. Juana couldn't help remembering that only two weeks ago her mother had been sitting on this rock cradling Anita in her arms.

"Look at those houses over there," Apá said as he pointed to a cluster of concrete houses. "Aren't they beautiful? See those little lights flickering on? They have electricity there, running water, and gas. When it rains, the houses never get flooded, and the roofs don't leak, and the people stay warm."

Juana counted the lights being turned on one at a time now that the sun was setting. On the other side of the sky, the silver horn-shaped moon was preparing to travel across the horizon.

"You see that blue one over there?" Apá asked. "Isn't that a beautiful house?"

Juana didn't look where Apá pointed, and neither did Amá. She didn't understand why he was doing this. In all the times they had come up here to watch the sunset, they had never talked about those houses. Those houses made of brick and concrete had never existed for them before. Only the stalks of corn swaying in the breeze, only the orange, red, and purple hues of the setting sun, only the river snaking its way around the mountains, had mattered.

Apá turned to look at them. "Answer me. Do you see those houses?"

Juana looked at Apá and nodded. "Sí, Apá, I see the houses."

Amá didn't respond.

"Wouldn't you like to live in one?"

Amá stood up and walked over to Apá. She put her arm around him and tried to turn him around. He didn't move.

"One day we will live in a house like that," he said.

"Sí viejo, algún día, but we must not think about that right now," Amá said.

Apá smiled for a moment, nodded slightly, then pointed at the stalks of corn now barely visible under the darkening sky. "Today I harvested corn from the bank of the river to all the way over there."

Juana tried to count the rows Apá was pointing to, but her eyes became blurry, and since she didn't want her father to see her cry, she quickly wiped her tears away.

adelina

Adelina hailed a taxicab at the airport and asked the driver to take her to a hotel. It was too late to catch a bus to the town. She would have to wait until daylight, only a few hours away.

Meanwhile, she looked out the taxicab window at the moon that followed her all the way from Los Angeles to Tijuana to now, through the dark streets of Mexico City. The ever-changing moon, her only faithful companion, she knew well after many years.

Adelina was nearly sixteen when she arrived in Los Angeles. She was there to look for her father. On her first night there she met a man who told her something she hadn't known about the moon.

She'd gotten off the Greyhound bus that afternoon, walked up Seventh Street, and continued walking, turning the corner here and there, not knowing where to go. She didn't know anyone. She didn't have much money left, and she had no idea where to begin looking for her father.

She sat on a park bench by a small lake to rest her feet.

She saw men playing soccer, women pushing their children on swings, couples jogging together, other men lying on the grass, sleeping. One by one they'd gone home, except for the men sleeping on the grass. They didn't go anywhere, and Adelina wondered if this was where they lived, and would they bother her if she stayed.

The moon that night was a crescent moon. By then Adelina already knew the moon had eight phases. Eight ways she presented herself to the world.

The reflection of the moon rippled in the water. The wind ruffled her hair and her stomach growled.

She couldn't bring herself to stand up and go look for food. She would sit there and wait until she was ready to pick herself up and start looking for her father. From the window of the Greyhound bus Adelina had noticed one thing: Los Angeles was a huge city. Where did one begin searching for a lost loved one in a city such as this?

She heard a strange rattling sound and turned to see a man pushing a shopping cart filled with cans and bottles. He rummaged through a trash bin down by the restrooms and took out a few cans. He slowly made his way down to her, whistling. It was a familiar song, but she was too hungry to think of its name.

The man stopped to look inside the trash bin near her bench. She tried to be completely still, hoping the man would not see her. But the man turned and saw her, and stopped whistling.

"Hay cabrón, you sure scared the hell out of me, girl. You look like a ghost."

"Lo siento," Adelina said.

"Now what are you doing at this hour of the night, alone?" the man asked while emptying the contents of a beer can.

"I'm looking at the moon," Adelina said. The man looked up at the sky and nodded.

"Yeah, sometimes it calls to you, doesn't it? It robs you of your sleep. I've stayed up watching it sometimes, too."

Adelina remained quiet. She could see the men across the lake getting up to look at her. She'd hoped they would stay sleeping on the grass.

"You want to know something about the moon?" the man asked.

Adelina nodded.

"It has two faces. She only shows one face to the world. Even though it changes shape constantly, it's always the same face we see. But her second face, her second face remains hidden in darkness. That's the face no one can see. People call it the dark side of the moon. Two identities. Two sides of a coin. Now isn't that interesting?"

"Yes, it's interesting," Adelina said.

"You know, you shouldn't be out here alone. It's dangerous. Don't you have a place to go?"

Adelina shook her head.

"Look, if you walk up Fourth Street, and turn left on Evergreen, you'll end up at a place that used to be a convent, but now it's an apartment building that looks like Dracula's castle. The rooms are small. They're dirty and full of roaches and mice, but the rent is cheap. And it's a lot better than being here in the park. When you get there ask for Don Ernesto, he's the manager. He's a nice man. Tell him Carlos sent you."

Adelina thought about the money she had in her pocket and wondered if it would be enough. But the man was right. She couldn't stay out here. She remembered the one time she'd tried to sleep on a park bench and had ended up in jail.

She grabbed her backpack and stood up to go, thanking the man who said his name was Carlos.

"Now you be careful girl. By the way, what's your name?"

"Adelina Vasquez."

juana

"Come with me, Juana. There's something I must tell you."

"What is it, Apá?"

Apá didn't reply. But when he put out his hand, Juana immediately reached out and grabbed it. His hand was rough like the pumice stones with which her mother cleaned the pots.

Juana walked by his side. The frown on his face told her she was to ask no questions. Dark clouds were gathering up above them, heavy with rain. Pebbles danced in and out of her sandals as they made their way alongside the river, past a cluster of shacks. They walked across the bridge. As they made their way through the rows of concrete houses on each side of the street, Juana kept her eyes aimed at the ground and didn't look up.

They walked up the street to the church. The last rays of the sun shone through the stained-glass windows and fell on the walls like a shattered rainbow. A woman sat on one of the pews humming an Ave María. Her head was covered with a black veil and a rosary hung from her hands.

Apá led Juana to the pew in front of La Virgen de Guadalupe. She stood on an altar wrapped in her blue mantle sprinkled with white stars. Apá fidgeted around in his seat. Then he grabbed Juana's hand and looked her straight in the eyes. His breath mingled with the scent of melted wax and withering flowers. The woman began chanting an Our Father and that's when Apá said, "In a few days I will leave for El Otro Lado."

Juana looked up at La Virgen de Guadalupe not knowing what to say. *Why would you leave us? Don't you love us anymore? Don't you love me anymore? Apá, Apá* . . . she thought, but said nothing. She listened to the woman's chant and found herself mumbling the prayer with her. "Hágase Tu voluntad en la tierra como en el cielo . . ." Let your will be done on Earth as it is in Heaven.

Why are you taking him away from me? Juana asked La Virgen.

"Don't think that I'm leaving forever, mi'ja. I'm only going away for a while to earn money." Apá pulled out a letter from his pocket. He didn't know how to read, and Juana wondered who'd read him the letter. "My friend has written to me from the other side. Here, read about the things he tells me."

Juana took the letter from her father's hand. As she read it, he mumbled the words along with her—he seemed to have already memorized them. Apá's friend wrote about riches unheard of, streets that never end, and buildings that nearly reach the sky. He wrote that there's so much money to be made, and so much food to eat, people there don't know what hunger is.

"Miguel, in one hour you can make the same amount of money you make working the whole day in Mexico."

"Can you imagine that, Juana?" Apá asked. "If what he says is true, it won't take me long to make money to build a real house."

"No, Apá, you can't leave us. You can't go away. We don't need a house like that. Please, I'm sorry about what I did. Please, Apá, don't go, don't go!"

Juana threw herself into her father's arms and held him tight.

"I'm sorry, my daughter, but working as a campesino, earning a few pesos a day, isn't enough. Do you understand?"

Juana looked down at the floor.

"I will come back as soon as I have enough money. I promise," Apá said.

"Is El Otro Lado far away, Apá?"

"It doesn't matter, mi'ja. That's the only way I can ever hope to make enough money to build a house for my family."

They made the sign of the cross and stood to go. Their footsteps echoed against the walls as they left. When they opened the door Juana turned to glance back at La Virgen de Guadalupe. She felt that La Virgen must have disappeared and left her, too, for she was now only clay, paint, and eyes of glass.

On their way home Apá stopped and put a hand on Juana's shoulder. He turned her to face the cornfields which stretched for several kilometers, their green color blending with the dark purple of the mountains rising high into the sky.

"Do you see the mountains over there at the far end of the fields?" Apá asked.

Juana nodded.

"El Otro Lado is over there, on the other side of those mountains."

"Really, Apá?"

"So you see, Juana," Apá said as he bent down to look at her. "I won't be that far from you. When you feel that you need to talk to your Apá, just look toward the mountains, and the wind will carry your words to me."

Juana looked at the mountains again. Maybe the mountains weren't that far away after all.

"Come, I'll race you to the house," he said.

As always, Apá stayed behind for a few seconds while Juana ran ahead. Soon, he caught up to her and took her hand. They ran down the street, Apá pulling her behind him like a kite. She knew they were almost home when the cobbled stones were replaced with dirt and pebbles. And the rows of pink, blue, yellow, purple, and green concrete houses became shacks growing out of the earth. Little shacks made out of bamboo sticks and cardboard, some leaning against one another like little old ladies tired after a long walk.

adelina

Don Ernesto decided he would adopt Adelina the moment he first laid eyes on her.

"You looked like a little bird lost in the dark," he would say whenever they talked about that night.

Adelina remembered she had stood outside the door of the apartment building, shivering. The night was cold and the hour late. Carlos had called this Dracula's castle, and now she saw why. The building was surrounded by so many trees and various kinds of bushes that it was barely visible through the branches. After what seemed a long time of knocking, she had given up and was already heading down the steps when someone opened the door.

"May I help you?" the old man asked as he poked his head out.

"I'm looking for a place to stay. Carlos sent me here to speak to Don Ernesto."

"I'm Don Ernesto. Come in, child. You'll catch your death standing outside in the cold."

Adelina let herself be guided down a dark hallway. A framed picture of La Virgen de Guadalupe hung on the wall above a candlelit table.

Don Ernesto made the sign of the cross as they walked by the frame. Adelina didn't look at it. She kept her eyes glued on Don Ernesto's back.

He took her up the stairs and led her to a room with the number twelve on the door.

"You're lucky this was vacated this morning. The family that lived here has moved on to Salinas, to work in the fields. They didn't have much luck here working in the factories." Don Ernesto switched on the light and motioned for Adelina to go inside the room. Roaches scurried, just like Carlos said. A roach passed by her foot, and she quickly squashed it.

"It's not much, but in these walls you'll be safe," Don Ernesto said. "Now go to sleep, child. Tomorrow we'll decide what you're going to do."

Adelina leaned against the closed door and listened to him walk away. What was she going to do? She was going to find her father.

juana

Apá bought a chicken at a downtown rotisserie in celebration of Juana's twelfth birthday. He knew it was Juana's favorite meal, and although he didn't have much money to spare, he'd wanted to give her this special surprise.

"I wish I could give you more, Juana," he said. Juana took a bite but found it hard to swallow. Apá was leaving early the next morning.

Amá was quiet, making only infrequent attempts to talk.

When everyone was silent, Juana could hear the rain landing on the cardboard roof. She could see the drops leaking through and falling in the pots on the floor. A drop fell on her cheek, but before she lifted her hand to wipe it, Apá had stretched his arm from across the table and wiped the water off her cheek.

"Soon," he said, "I'll get us out of this shack." He looked up at the roof and said, "I hate this house." He said it softly, but Juana still heard him.

• • •

At night, when Apá tucked Juana into bed, she asked him for a story. It had been a long time since he had told her one. But, ever since her sister drowned, Juana had not asked. Apá liked to hold Anita on his lap while he told both of them a story, and Juana had not wanted to look at Apá's empty lap.

But tonight she hungered for his every word, smile, touch. She knew this would be the last story he told her before he left.

"All right, Juana. What story would you like to hear?"

"My favorite one," she said. "About the grapes."

Apá pulled up a chair and sat beside Juana's cot. Amá untied the curtain hanging from the ceiling and pulled it across the room, as if to hide behind it.

"When I was seven years old," Apá began, "my father took me to the vineyards for the first time. He gave me a knife and told me to cut only the ripe purple grapes. We would be working from sunup to sundown, cutting grapes row by row, filling up basket after basket. He pointed to a row and told me to start there. I tried to work fast because I wanted my father to be proud. I quickly filled my basket and took it to my father. I could barely carry it because it was so full."

"And was your Apá proud?" Juana asked.

"Well," Apá continued, "when I let the basket fall in front of my father, he looked at it and gasped. 'What have you done?' he asked. 'What have you done?'" Apá paused.

What had he done?

"'You cut the wrong grapes. I told you to cut the ripe purple ones,' my father said. 'I did,' I told him. I grabbed a bunch and held it up close to his face, but he slapped the grapes from my hand and said that I had cut the green grapes. I looked at them, and I wondered why he was saying that. 'You cut the green grapes,' my father said again, and he sent me home."

"And then what happened?" Juana asked, pretending not to know. "Did you cut the green grapes or the purple ones?"

"My father was right. I had cut the green grapes, but I didn't know it."

"How could you not know what's purple or green?"

She remembered when she first saw Apá wear a blue sock and a green sock. And sometimes Amá would giggle when he would wear different-colored clothes that didn't match. "You look like a flag," she would say. And one time Amá asked him to buy red, ripe tomatoes at the market and Apá brought some that were a sickly shade of orange.

"Well, you see," Apá said. "I can't see colors the right way."

Juana lifted her arms and Apá responded by leaning toward her and hugging her. "I'm sorry," Juana said.

Apá leaned back and asked, "About what, Juana?"

"About making you tell me a story. I know it—"

"Hush, mi'ja. It is your birthday."

Juana was awake even before the roosters crowed. She lay in her cot listening to the rain outside and the uneven snores of Amá and Apá.

Soon, she heard them stirring awake, and she knew the hour had come for her father to leave.

"It's raining again."

Juana heard Amá's whisper in the darkness. Amá didn't

light a candle, but when Juana saw a spark on the other side of
the shack, she knew Amá was going to make coffee. She heard
her blowing puffs of air to light the coals in the brazier.

A chair squeaked. When Amá lit the candles Juana could
see Apá sitting next to her mother. He put up his hands near
the glowing coals to warm them.

"I told Don Elías that in four weeks I will send him his
money," Apá said.

"And what did he say, Miguel?" Amá asked.

Don Elías was the owner of the mortuary. He had pro-
vided everything for Anita's funeral: the coffin, the flowers, the
candles, the mass, and the truck that carried all the elderly
people, and anyone else who was too weak to walk, to the
cemetery. Juana wondered how much money Apá owed Don
Elías. Not long ago, he had finally finished paying for María's
funeral from when she died four years ago.

"He'll wait," Apá said. "I'll work hard as soon as I get there
so that I can pay him. You know how he is, Lupe." Apá sighed,
then said, "Remember how hard it was last time?"

They were quiet for a moment. Then Amá went to open the
drawer of the dresser by their cot. She put Apá's clothes into her
only shopping bag. The bag smelled of onions, chiles, cilantro,
and garlic and a faint scent of jasmine. It smelled of Amá. The
smell would soak into his clothes and Juana knew the next time
Apá wore them in El Otro Lado, he would think of Amá.

Apá took one more drink of his coffee and stood to go. He
walked over to Juana. She closed her eyes and pretended she
was asleep. Then she felt his lips press against her cheek. His
breath was warm on her face, like when Amá boiled beans and

Juana would lift the lid of the pot once in a while to smell them. The vapor would cover her face, promising a good meal to come.

When her face felt cold again, she knew Apá had already walked away. She lay in her cot, fighting back her tears. She couldn't help but think that it was her fault Apá was leaving.

She grabbed her rosary from under the pillow and then went outside.

In the darkness, she could barely see Apá making his way to the bridge. The rain beat down on him, and he kept his head hanging low, as if seeking forgiveness from it.

"He's leaving us," Amá said, crying.

Juana broke into a run, trying to catch up to her father. The rain pasted her hair over her eyes, and she was blindfolded, as if she were about to break a piñata at a birthday party.

"Apá! Apá!"

Apá turned around and waited for her.

"Take this. It'll keep you safe."

Juana placed her rosary on Apá's calloused hand and then closed his fingers over it.

Amá shivered as a gust of wind blew in through the gaps between the bamboo sticks. She sat on the dirt floor with her eyes closed. Juana lay on her cot. Apá had been gone for six hours now, and neither she nor Amá had felt like doing anything. Juana wondered what Amá was thinking. She looked scared and worried. Was she afraid Apá would forget her once he got to El Otro Lado?

Sometimes Juana and her mother would see women sitting

by the door, embroidering servilletas while waiting outside for the mailman, waiting for the letter from El Otro Lado that rarely, sometimes never, came. Those were the forgotten women, the abandoned women. *But Amá mustn't worry about that,* Juana thought. *Apá would never forget her. He would never abandon us.*

The door suddenly opened and Apá's mother, Abuelita Elena, walked in. She looked at Juana still in bed and at Amá sitting on the floor, leaning against the wall. Amá slowly opened her eyes and turned to look at Abuelita Elena. Her eyes squinted at the bright light.

Abuelita Elena's old age made her body stoop to the ground. Her silver hair was braided and twisted atop her head like a crown.

"Lupe, what are you doing there on the ground and your kid still under the blankets? It's twelve o'clock already. Get up, both of you. Stop lying there like donkeys."

Amá didn't move. Her swollen eyelids closed over her eyes and shut Abuelita Elena out. Abuelita Elena walked to the bed and tried to yank the blanket out from under Juana.

"Lazy child. Lupe, you useless woman. My son has gone to a strange country to support you and your chamaca and all you do is sit on your lazy nalgas the whole day and cry? You chased my son away. You, with your carelessness." Abuelita Elena glared at Amá. "My son. He came yesterday to say good-bye to me. 'Adiós Amá,' he said, and then he left. These bones are old and soon I will die without ever seeing him again. My only son. It's your fault, Lupe."

Amá didn't answer.

"Leave her alone," Juana said. "It's not her fault Apá left. It's mine. You leave my mother alone."

"You insolent child. You'll end up just like your mother, a beggar in the streets, trying to leech on someone."

"Get out of here, señora." Amá got to her feet and pointed at the door.

"What did you say?" Abuelita Elena walked toward Amá.

"I said get out. It's true you've never accepted me as your son's wife, but you have no right to come and insult me or my daughter."

"I still can't understand how my son got involved with a woman like you," Abuelita Elena said. "An orphaned beggar who—"

Amá grabbed a pot filled with rainwater and threw it at Abuelita Elena. The pot landed at Abuelita Elena's feet and the water splashed on her dress. "Get out of my house!" Amá yelled.

Abuelita Elena's hunched figure turned to leave. Her eyes roamed around the shack, resting on the pots Amá had placed around the room to catch the rainwater. She looked at the brazier and the gray coals, the dresser with the two missing drawers, the altar, the wooden table in the corner adorned with the withering branches of the cilantro Amá had put inside a cup with water. She looked at the clay mug filled with the cold coffee Apá had not finished drinking.

"You'll be an abandoned woman, Lupe," she sneered. And she turned and walked away.

Juana's godmother came a few hours later to console Amá. "Ay, comadre," she said, "I just can't believe my compadre is gone. It must be so hard for you."

Amá broke into fresh tears and let herself be pulled against Antonia's large bosom. "He's gone, comadre, Miguel is gone."

Once her tears subsided Amá told Antonia what Abuelita Elena had said that morning. Juana had never understood why Abuelita Elena hated her mother so much. But her godmother explained that Abuelita Elena had been trying to marry her only son to an older spinster woman who had inherited a nice house and good money from her father. But then Apá met Amá. She was walking around the street selling boxes of gum. She had been dressed in tattered clothes, her face covered with soot and dirt, yet Apá had fallen in love with her.

"There, there, Lupe. Don't pay attention to what that woman says," Antonia said. "He will soon come back, you'll see. And he will build you a nice house, with a stove and a refrigerator."

"That's not important, Antonia," Amá said. "What matters is that we pay Don Elías his money back soon. I don't like owing him anything. You know how he was last time, charging Miguel so much interest."

"Yes, I remember how hard my compadre worked to repay him."

Juana tried to busy herself mending the tears on her dresses, but she was attentive to every word she heard. She remembered the last time her father had been in debt. He had walked around bent over, as if he was carrying a heavy sack of corn he'd just harvested in the fields.

When he finally finished paying the last peso, he stood straight again and walked around town with his head held high, once more a free man.

"It worries me, Antonia." Amá was whispering as if she didn't want Juana to hear.

"Most people owe him, Lupe, and that gives him power,

especially with the judiciales. Don't you remember he had them arrest Cesar a month ago? And all because Cesar picked some lemons off Don Elías's lemon tree!"

"That was just an excuse," Amá said. "You know Don Elías was after Cesar's sister. That's why he sent the police after Cesar, so he could get her alone."

Juana pricked her thumb, having taken her eyes off the needle. Everyone knew Don Elías was always after some woman in town. She wondered what his wife thought about that. Juana had only seen Don Elías's wife a few times. She rarely came out of her house. She was a thin, pale woman, already in her forties, and had no children. She never smiled. Some of the women would go to her to beg her to protect their husbands, brothers, or fathers from Don Elías's wrath. But she never said or did anything. She just sat there, knitting baby clothes she donated to the church, silent.

Juana put the needle and the dress she was mending on the table, and went outside. She didn't want to hear any more. She knew what she had done. By falling asleep, not only had she killed her own sister, but she had buried her father beneath the weight of the debt owed to Don Elías.

Juana and Amá spent the rest of the day on their knees praying for Apá's safety, and praying for Anita's soul. Juana wondered if her sister was now an angel in Heaven, and if she was, she hoped Anita would watch over Apá.

When darkness fell, their throats were aching for water, and their empty bellies were crying for food. With one last prayer, Amá finally grabbed hold of the altar and lifted herself up.

"Come to the table, Juana. It's time to eat."

Juana sat on the table while Amá filled a cup of water for her from the clay pot. Juana wet her dry lips first, and then took a long drink from her cup. Amá headed to the brazier to light the coals. She warmed the hard tortillas left over from last night's meal, the last meal they'd shared with Apá.

"Juana, go outside and get some chili peppers from the plant," Amá said.

Juana did as she was told. The cool night air dried the sweat on her forehead. She listened to the gentle rushing of the river farther down, the crickets' song of sorrow and longing, the rustling of the trees, the hooting of a lechuza on the roof of the shack.

She held her breath. What was that owl doing here?

She felt for the chili peppers with her fingers and quickly yanked them from the plant. Then she ran back into the shack, hoping Amá had not heard the owl's hoots. Owls always brought bad news. News of death.

For the first time since she was a little girl, Juana slept with Amá. Her warm body next to her calmed her fears, and maybe, just maybe, Amá's warmth would chase away the demons that had taken Juana's sleep away.

But it wasn't so. Amá stirred in the cot just as Juana was beginning to fall asleep. The springs squeaked as Amá got up. Juana wondered what she was going to do. Amá headed to the wardrobe and took out a cardboard box. She laid it on the table before walking to the altar to grab two candles. She put the candles on the table and then sat down.

Juana knew what was in the box. It contained the set of

plates Amá had received as a gift when she and Apá got married. Amá was orphaned at an early age and was raised by her godmother until she was twelve years old, when her godmother passed away. She was fourteen when she met Apá.

Amá said that she and Apá fell in love at first sight. They wanted to marry but they couldn't afford to pay for the ceremony. One day, Governor Rubén Figueroa said that anyone who wanted to get married could go to the ayuntamiento and marry for free, and they would receive a set of plates as a wedding gift.

For thirteen years now, that box of plates had sat in the wardrobe. Amá refused to use it, saying that one day, when Juana got married, the set would be hers.

"It gave me and your father good luck, Juana. We've had a good marriage," Amá always said.

Now Juana watched her mother take out the cups one by one. They were adorned with imprints of purple lilacs and pink butterflies. Amá ran her fingers over their smooth, white silkiness and kissed them before setting them down on the table. Juana felt as if she were intruding upon her mother, so she turned around and closed her eyes.

She thought about the plates, shining so prettily under the candlelight, and tried to forget the tears she saw gathering in her mother's eyes.

Apá had been gone for only two days when Don Elías came knocking on the door. Juana opened it and stood almost at eye level with him. He was a short, fat man who reminded Juana of a gorilla she had once seen in a book. His shirt was unbuttoned almost halfway down his chest, exposing hundreds of black hairs stuck together with sweat. Juana wished he would button his shirt before Amá spoke with him. There was something indecent about the bulges of fat beneath those hairs.

Don Elías wiped the sweat running down his puffy cheeks. He cleared his throat and said, "Is your mother home?"

Juana turned to look at Amá, hesitating to say who had come. She was on the ground, leaning over a metate grinding a handful of dry corn.

"Well, is she home, yes or no?"

"Who is it, Juana?" Amá asked.

"It's me, Lupe. Elías!" he called out.

Juana watched as Don Elías straightened the collar of his shirt but did not button it.

Amá came to the door. "How can I help you?" she asked.

Don Elías looked past Amá, as if hoping she would ask him to come in. Amá stood her ground, blocking the doorway.

"Ah, well, I just wanted to come and say how sorry I am your husband has left for El Otro Lado. I know you're all alone now with your daughter, and I wanted to offer—"

"Don't worry, Don Elías, my daughter and I will be fine. As for your money, my husband promised to send it in a few weeks, and I will inform you when it arrives."

Don Elías cleared his throat and ran his fingers through his sweaty, graying hair. "Yes, yes, Doña Lupe, that'll be fine. Do inform me when you receive news of your husband."

"Yes, I will certainly do that, now good day to you," Amá said. Don Elías didn't turn to leave. Instead, he stood there looking at Amá, his eyes narrowing to slits. It reminded Juana of the way a cat looks at a bird before it prepares to pounce on it. Now what business did Don Elías have looking at Amá like that?

"Miguel said in four weeks he'll be sending the money, right?" he asked.

"That's right, Don Elías, in four weeks."

"Very well. I will return then."

Amá closed the door as soon as Don Elías left.

Juana's stomach hurt, as if she had swallowed a hot coal that was now burning a hole inside her.

When they finished their evening meal of tortillas and dried cheese, Juana went outside to rinse the plates with rainwater from the barrel by the door. She glanced in the direction of the fields, and even though she couldn't see them through the trees, she tried to imagine that Apá was there, harvesting corn. Soon he would be coming home.

Juana shivered. There was that owl again, perched on the tree in front of her. She could hear its hoots, soft like a lament.

"Get out of here!" Juana yelled. She put the plates down and picked up stones from the ground. "Get out. Leave!"

She ran toward the tree, throwing the stones as hard as she could.

Juana watched her mother combing her long thick hair in the darkness. Amá sat on Juana's cot, and Juana was glad that now Amá would be sleeping beside her every night. She needed to be able to touch her mother—she was so afraid of losing her, too. The look Don Elías had given Amá bothered her still. She had seen other men look at Amá like that when they went to el mercado, or on their way to church or the cemetery. Even when they went to the plaza accompanied by Apá.

"Why are you still standing there, Juana? Come to bed." Amá patted the cot, motioning her to come sit beside her. Juana closed the door, put the dishes on the table, and went to her mother. She took the comb from Amá and breathed in the scent of jasmine that enveloped her.

As Juana brushed her mother's hair, the light of the moon streamed through the cracks of the shack in tiny shafts.

adelina

"Adelina? Is that you?"

Adelina clutched the phone receiver tight in her hand. Perhaps she shouldn't have called so late. It was four in the morning. But she'd wanted to hear a familiar voice. She felt so alone in this strange city.

"Yes, it's me, Maggie."

"Where are you? We've been so worried about you. Dr. Clark said you'd called to say you had an emergency and would be gone for a few weeks. I went to your apartment a few times and couldn't find you. Are you all right?"

"Yes, everything's fine. I'm in Mexico City," Adelina said as she leaned back against the pillow.

"You're in Mexico?"

"Yes."

"But what are you doing over there?"

"I'll explain things when I get back. How's everyone?"

"They're hanging in there. I went to visit Diana today.

She's doing really well. She told me she's looking into a job. I'm really glad she pulled through. There was a time when I thought she wouldn't."

"Yes, me, too. Keep an eye on her for me, Maggie."

"I'll do that. When are you coming back to Los Angeles?"

Adelina looked around her hotel room. She saw herself reflected in the dresser mirror across the room, opposite the bed. She looked at the cross hanging above the headboard.

"I don't know yet, Maggie."

After a pause, Maggie said, "Dr. Luna came by the shelter yesterday. He asked about you."

Adelina grabbed the rosary from the nightstand and gently rubbed the beads.

"I told him you'd gone on vacation," Maggie continued. "Adelina, why won't you tell me what made you end your relationship with him? I mean, everything was going so well between you—"

"Listen, Maggie. I've got to go now. I'm sorry about waking you up so late."

"We miss you at the shelter. Come back soon."

"I'll try, Maggie. Good night."

After she put the phone down, Adelina grabbed her purse and fished out her bottle of sleeping pills. She popped two pills in her mouth and washed them down with water. Then she covered herself with the comforter, hoping the sleeping pills would work quickly and plunge her into a dreamless sleep.

juana

Whenever Juana and Amá went to town, whispers floated all around them. Juana heard the words clearly. The women said things to each other, being careful to put a hand over their mouths as if to muffle the words.

"He's been gone for four weeks now, and he hasn't sent word."

"Has he abandoned them, you think?"

"No, Miguel is an honest man. He wouldn't do such a thing."

"Honest or not, once they find themselves in El Otro Lado, surrounded by all those golden-haired gringas, a man cannot help himself."

"Poor Doña Lupe," they said, and smirked.

Juana covered her ears and tried hard not to listen. But the words always came chasing them, barking louder than the stray dogs wandering around the streets.

• • •

Unbeknownst to Amá, Juana had been skipping school. She'd get up and drink coffee with her mother. She walked with her alongside the river, across the bridge, and followed the train tracks to town. But once the tracks parted, one going to the station and the other in the direction of school, Juana kissed her mother good-bye and hid behind a guamúchil tree until Amá disappeared from sight. She was heading to the train station where she now worked selling quesadillas.

Juana was tired of the kids taunting her, making a mockery out of her pain.

"Your father abandoned you," they said. "Poor, poor Juana, what would she do now without her papi?"

Juana was already used to being laughed at. The kids made fun of her for being twelve years old and still in the fourth grade. But Apá always told her not to listen. It wasn't her fault that sometimes he didn't have money to buy the books and materials she needed for school. And it definitely wasn't her fault when the dirt roads were so muddy during the rainy season that it was difficult for anyone living in the outskirts to get into town.

But now Apá wasn't here to make her feel better about the kids teasing her. And in a way, it was because of him they were now laughing at her. Juana wasn't the only kid whose father or mother had left for El Otro Lado. But at least they had not been forgotten, like her.

Juana would run back home and sit outside to wait for the mailman, although he seldom came. Sometimes she would go down to Don Agustín's house because he and his wife lived closer to town. She thought that maybe in his laziness, the mailman had opted to leave Apá's letter with them. But it was never so.

Maybe today the letter has come, Juana thought as she made her way down to Don Agustín's house. His wife, Doña Martina, was a tiny woman wrapped in a gray rebozo. She sat outside watching Juana walk toward her shack.

"Buenas tardes, Juana," Doña Martina said. In her hand she held an old comb that had some missing teeth. She looked at Juana and smiled. Her gap-toothed smile reminded Juana of her comb.

"Good afternoon, Doña Martina. Has the mailman come by today?"

Doña Martina struggled with the tangles in her hair. As usual, she handed her comb to Juana.

"The mailman hasn't come today, mi'ja. I'm sorry."

Juana took the comb from her and walked around the chair to stand behind her. From inside Doña Martina's shack she could hear the soft cooing of doves and smell the scent of herbs and almond oil. Doña Martina was a healer and midwife. She'd helped Amá deliver her children.

"Perhaps tomorrow the letter will get here, Juana. You must be patient. Sometimes letters take a long time to arrive."

Juana looked toward the mountains. Apá said he would be on the other side, not far away. So why was it taking so long for his letter to come? Unless he had not sent it. Tears threatened to come out of her eyes, and Juana wished Doña Martina wouldn't see.

But Doña Martina seemed to smell Juana's sadness like the way she could smell the air and know that rain is coming. She grabbed Juana's hand and pulled her around so that she stood in front of her. Doña Martina's face was wrinkled and hard like chicharrones, and she smelled of almond oil, epazote, and cigarette smoke.

"You need to be strong, Juana, for your mother. I've noticed she has not been looking well. Is she ill?"

"My mother's fine," Juana said, although Doña Martina probably knew she was lying. For a few days now, Amá had been getting up early and going outside to vomit. Amá said it was because her body would swell with so much sadness throughout the night, that in the morning she just had to rid her stomach of it. "Sadness is poison, Juana," Amá told her.

Doña Martina stood up and went to gather some herbs growing outside her shack. "Here, Juana, take these herbs to your mother and tell her to make herself some tea. It will help her."

"Thank you, Doña Martina." Juana wondered if she should talk to Doña Martina about Amá's sickness. But deep down, she herself didn't want to know what Amá had. It wasn't just sadness that was making Amá sick. Juana knew that.

"The things that people say about you, Miguel, they aren't true. They say you won't write. They say you have abandoned me. But it isn't so, I know."

Juana watched her mother caressing her pretty plates. She tried to close her eyes, or look elsewhere, but her eyes always returned to Amá sitting on the ground in front of the altar. Amá put one plate down and picked up another, demanding answers from it. "Where are you, Miguel? Why don't you write? Where are you, mi amor? No me olvides."

Juana echoed Amá's words. Where are you, Apá?

Don't forget me.

Don Elías came knocking on their door on the fifth week after Apá left, just like Amá said he would. She had managed to save twenty pesos from working at the station. She had opened her hand and showed him the coins, but Don Elías had only laughed at her.

"I will pay you every cent," Amá told him. "I swear I will, but you must give my husband time."

"It's strange, is it not, señora, that he has sent no word to you of his whereabouts. Perhaps he has forgotten his responsibilities."

"Don't say that!" Juana said. "Apá would never do such a thing. You—"

"Hasn't your mother taught you not to interrupt your elders, girl?" Don Elías asked, looking at Amá, who blushed with embarrassment. Juana cowered into a corner, knowing she had shamed her mother by forgetting her manners. But he had no right to speak so ill of her father!

"My husband knows his responsibilities, Don Elías. And he's not a man to forget them."

"I'm sure you're right, Lupe, but if things turn out differently, I will be willing to make another kind of arrangement." Don Elías's eyes narrowed as he smiled at Amá. Juana recognized the look.

Amá was quiet for a moment and then said, "Forgive me, Don Elías, but if you won't accept my humble payment, then I must ask you to leave."

Before he could reply, Amá closed the door on him and leaned against it, as if afraid he would try to knock it down. She breathed deeply and slowly to calm herself. She opened her hand and looked at the metal coins in her palm.

Juana knew how hard she had worked for them. But she also knew they would never be enough.

adelina

Adelina boarded the bus at ten in the morning. It would be a three-hour ride to her destination. She found a seat by the window and sat down. She looked at the faces of the people boarding the bus. The faces of strangers. A woman wrapped in a blue shawl. A man with a thick, black mustache on his face and a Tejano hat on his head. A woman wearing sunglasses and red lipstick. A young man with a slightly crooked nose and eyes that drooped, making him seem sad.

Adelina watched the young man as he looked around for an empty seat. Once he sat down a few seats in front of her she could no longer see him. There was something familiar about him. His was not the face of a stranger. It was the face of a person she hadn't seen in a long time. Those droopy eyes. Whom did they remind her of?

"You're going to visit someone?" the man sitting next to her asked. Adelina turned to look at the man. "I mean, you aren't from here, right?"

She smiled faintly. She didn't know what to say. She was from here, and yet she wasn't. How could she explain?

"You came from El Otro Lado. I could see that right away," the man said, smiling.

"I'm going to see my mother," Adelina said, looking down at the wooden box on her lap.

"Oh, that's a good thing. When was the last time you saw her?"

"Many years ago."

"That's too bad," the man said. "But you're glad to be back, right? You're finally going home."

She thought about what the man said. Was she really going home?

She recalled the conversation she had with the old coyote.

"Why did you help me find my father?" she had asked him while they sat in the immigration office waiting to fill out the paperwork so she could claim her father's body.

"So that you can go home," the old man said, again.

He'd told her the same thing the day he'd followed her to the hotel.

"I don't understand what you mean," Adelina said. Did he not want to admit he'd heard about the reward she was offering to anyone who would help her find her father?

The old man looked intently at her, and she had a feeling he could see more clearly with his blind eye than with his good eye. She felt that eye exposed her, in its blindness, it saw her for who she really was.

"You don't remember me, do you?" the old man asked.

Adelina looked at him more closely. She knew there was

something familiar about him, about the sound of his voice, his blind eye. Perhaps she'd met him long ago. She'd met so many men.

"Do I know you?" she asked.

The old man looked down at the linoleum floor. Adelina felt that he had suddenly become embarrassed. He cleared his throat before he spoke again.

"Many years ago, you once held me in your arms. And while I tried to find comfort in your embrace you said something to me, something that made me run away from you. You said, 'I am looking for my father. He came to cross the border three years ago.'

"You described to me a man I remembered well. You said he had a white rosary with him. A rosary with heart-shaped beads."

Adelina brought her hand up to her mouth and bit her thumb hard. Her jaw trembled slightly.

"I didn't have the courage to tell you then that I had buried your father in the middle of the border. You were so young, and all you wanted was to go back home." The old man grabbed her hand. He struggled to get down on the floor and then knelt in front of her. "Forgive me, child, forgive this old man for being a coward. I was afraid. I was afraid they would say I killed him."

Adelina looked at him, remembering how sixteen years ago he had run away from her and had never returned. She had been so close to knowing the truth back then. She had searched for him for weeks, on every street, in every bar. Every man who passed her by, she would look to see if he had a blue film over his left eye.

"Do you forgive this old man?"

Adelina looked at the old man's blind eye and swallowed the bile in her mouth.

juana

Don Elías came back the following week. Juana was on her way to the tortilla mill when she saw him walking across the bridge, heading toward her house. She felt like turning around and running back to warn Amá he was coming, but she knew Amá was hungry, and she also knew if she didn't hurry, she might find the tortilla mill closed for the day. She had no choice but to keep walking alongside the river and try to keep herself calm.

"Buenas tardes, Juanita, is your mother home?" Don Elías asked.

"Sí, señor," Juana said, immediately wishing she had lied.

"Good, good."

Juana took off running down to the bridge. She decided to get back home as quickly as she could. Surely her mother would not like being alone with that fat pig. She got to the tortilla mill panting.

"Calm down, Juana, what's the rush?" Doña Hortencia asked as soon as she got there.

"Nothing, Doña Hortencia."

"How's your mother, Juana? Have you heard from your father yet?"

"Give me half a kilo of tortillas, please," Juana said, ignoring her question. She looked behind at the women who were grabbing the hot tortillas as they came out of the press. Nosy women. But she wouldn't give them any reason to go gossiping again about Amá and Apá.

"Well, here you are," Doña Hortencia said in an angry tone. She slammed the hot tortillas down on the counter, on top of Juana's hand.

"Ouch!" Juana cried. The women behind Doña Hortencia giggled. She threw the pesos on the counter, put the tortillas inside her basket, and ran out of the mill.

The first thing Juana saw when she got home was Don Elías pinning Amá against the wall.

"Don't make me do anything bad to you, señora," he was telling Amá. "I can go get the judiciales and have them arrest you for failing to pay your debt to me."

"No, señor, please, just give me one more week, I'm sure my husband will—"

"Your husband has turned out to be an irresponsible hijo de la chingada! He—"

"Don't you insult my father!" Juana took a step toward Don Elías, ready to throw the tortillas at him.

Amá turned to look at her. Juana noticed the beads of sweat gathering above her mother's upper lip.

"Juana, go outside," she said.

"But Amá—"

"Now!"

"Go on, girl, do as your mother says," Don Elías said, smirking.

Juana slammed the basket of tortillas on the table and headed to the door. She stopped in the doorway and turned to look back at Don Elías and Amá. Her stomach heaved.

Don Elías was pressing his huge belly against her mother.

"Now, as I was saying, señora, there are other ways we can arrange for you to pay back your debt . . ."

Juana covered her ears and ran out of the shack. She sat on a large rock in front and waited for Don Elías to come out. Why was he bothering her mother so much? Couldn't he understand Apá would be sending the money soon? All the things people said, about her father having abandoned them, were not true. He was an honest man, and he would never forget her and Amá. He wouldn't.

"Get out of my house!" Amá yelled.

Something broke inside the shack, and soon after, Don Elías came out, yelling.

"I give you one week, Lupe, one week to think about it. The next time I come I won't be so generous with my offer!"

He left without even noticing Juana sitting there on the rock. She ran into the shack and found her mother on the floor, crying. She carefully stepped over the shards of glass scattered near the door.

"He said he's going to tell everyone in town to not give me work. I can't lose my job at the train station, Juana, how will we eat?"

Juana sat next to Amá and gently pulled back the strands of black hair covering her mother's face.

"Apá will soon be writing to us, you'll see," Juana said. Amá clung to Juana's words, nodded her head, and smiled faintly before breaking into tears again.

The next day Juana went to town to visit her grandmother. She found her sitting under the shade of the bougainvillea vine in her patio, dozing off. Her head fell forward, and she snapped it back against the back of the chair as she snored.

"Abuelita," Juana called, but her grandmother continued snoring. "Abuelita!"

Abuelita Elena trembled awake. She looked around and glared at Juana when she saw her standing by the gate.

"I came to ask about Apá." Juana walked in and went to stand beside her grandmother.

"Did your mother send you, huh?" Abuelita Elena asked. "What does she care about my son? All she ever did was make his life miserable with her lack of skills. 'Mi'jo,' I said to my son, 'that woman is not for you. She can't cook. She can't clean.' She can't even take proper care of children. Look at how many children have died. And who suffers most? My son. It is my son who has to work like a burro to repay his debts.

"But did he listen to me? No, all your father saw were her big tits and that big culo she likes to shake when she walks."

Juana bit her lips to keep from shouting at Abuelita Elena that her mother never did such things. But she knew if she angered her, Abuelita Elena would not give her any news. "Abuelita, have you heard from my father?"

Abuelita Elena glared at her, not saying anything. Juana wondered if she would be cruel enough to keep things from her.

"Please, Abuelita, please tell me if you have heard from him."

Abuelita Elena's bottom lip trembled slightly. "I have not, child. I have received no news of my son. It is as if the earth has swallowed him."

Juana didn't know what to say. She had been hoping to hear something else. She thanked her grandmother and turned to leave.

"And tell that mother of yours to stop sending you for information. I told him she would be the death of him, but he didn't listen. He didn't listen to his mother. And now he's gone. Where's my son? Where's my son?"

Abuelita Elena covered her face with her hands. Juana tiptoed back out to the gate, and closed it behind her when she left.

Don Elías was true to his word. When Amá showed up at the train station to help Doña Rosa with the food stand, she was told she could no longer work there.

"Forgive me, Lupe, please," Doña Rosa said. "It's just that you know Don Elías was kind enough to cover the funeral expenses when my mother died and, well, he said if I didn't do what he said he would force me to pay him everything I still owe him. It's nothing personal, Lupe, perdóname. But here, take these quesadillas with you, give some to Juana."

When Amá told Juana this, Juana didn't want to eat the quesadillas. Her stomach growled its complaint, having taken in only a piece of bread and watery coffee for breakfast.

"We can't afford to be proud, mi'ja," Amá said, but the quesadillas were left on the table the whole day. At night, when they both sat down to eat stale tortillas with green peppers, they stayed on the table, until Amá threw them away the next day.

For the next few days, Amá walked around town looking for a job, but everyone just shook their heads. As Don Elías predicted, everyone owed him one favor or another.

"Ay, comadre, there must be something you can do to earn money," Antonia told Amá.

"I've asked everywhere, Antonia," Amá said. "I've even asked people if I could wash and iron clothes for them, for a very low price, too, but they've said no."

"Don't worry, Lupe, I will help you as much as I can. What little food my husband brings home I'll share with you and my goddaughter."

"Thank you, comadre," Amá said. "But I won't take things from you. I won't be a burden to anyone. Juana and I will manage. Somehow."

"You need to take care of yourself, comadre. Especially now that you're alone."

"We'll be all right. One way or another, we will manage."

adelina

Adelina met Dr. Sebastian Luna at the General Hospital. One of the women who'd stayed at the shelter had recently gone back to her husband, and he'd beaten her again soon after. She'd called Maggie from the hospital to tell her what had happened. Maggie and Adelina went to see her.

"Laura, everything is going to be fine, you'll see," Maggie said as she held Laura's hand. Laura shook her head and kept crying.

"I don't know why he does it. I know he loves me. It's the alcohol he drinks. It makes him lose his head. . . ."

Adelina walked to the window behind the screen and looked outside. She'd started working at the shelter a few days ago. Before that, she worked at the Centro de Ayuda in Boyle Heights, and before that, she'd done volunteer work teaching a literacy class at the Downtown Women's Center while she finished school. And yet, despite many years of helping battered women, it was still difficult for her to look at Laura's bruised face.

There was a knock on the door, and Adelina heard someone come into the room.

"Good afternoon, Dr. Luna. Nice to see you," Maggie said.

"Nice to see you, too, Maggie. How's everyone doing at the shelter?"

"They're all hanging in there, Doctor."

Adelina stood still, one hand holding on to the curtain. Through the screen, she could barely see the doctor standing by Laura's bed. She moved to the side and saw him checking Laura's injuries. She noticed the lines of his hands, and the curve of his lips when he smiled.

"You're going to be as good as new in a few days," he told Laura.

As he stood up to go, Dr. Luna looked up.

"This is Adelina," Maggie said as she motioned for Adelina to come closer. She went to stand by Maggie's side. "She just started working at the shelter a few days ago."

Dr. Luna reached out to shake her hand. "Nice to meet you," he said. "I'm Sebastian Luna."

"Adelina Vasquez."

"It's a pleasure, Ms. Vasquez."

"He's one of the doctors who volunteer at the shelter," Maggie said. "He goes there twice a month."

Dr. Luna excused himself from the room. Adelina stared at the closed door. She could still see Dr. Luna's young face, and the way his green eyes had looked at her.

juana

Juana rummaged through the wooden crates the vendors had thrown away before closing their stalls at the marketplace. She found a few soggy tomatoes and chili peppers that were beginning to mold. Four homeless boys were also searching for food. The flies dancing around the rotting fruit and vegetables, and the dogs sniffing in the crates scattered around, competed with Juana and the boys. One of the boys jumped inside a trash bin to look for meat. He poked his head out of the trash bin and sighed. He held up chicken bones and blobs of fat.

"Look!" he yelled as he lifted his arm and pointed. A blob of fat fell from his hand and landed on Juana's shoulder. It looked like flan.

Juana turned and saw a stray dog pulling a chicken out of a crate. She knew the meat was spoiled, but despite herself, her mouth began to water. The boys chased after the dog, and she quickly followed behind them.

When the dog saw them coming, it picked up the chicken

and ran away. Juana and the boys chased the dog a few blocks, until it ran into someone's yard and hid.

"We almost had it," one of the boys said.

Juana went back to the mercado and picked up some shriveled carrots and a cabbage from a crate. She would ask Amá to make soup for dinner.

Dusk was falling by the time Juana neared her house. She stopped walking and looked at the mountains silhouetted against the orange-streaked sky. She thought about her father and wondered what he was doing. She looked at the cornstalks and thought about how much Amá loved eating corn roasted on the brazier. She looked down at the moldy vegetables in her hands and wished she was bringing her mother something better.

Juana threw the vegetables on the ground and ran all the way down to the river and then walked over the fallen tree that connected one side to the other. She soon found herself in the fields. The cornstalks swayed all around her, rocking the ears of corn as if they were babies. She slowly made her way through the rows, trying to be as quiet as possible.

Darkness had fallen quickly, and she could barely see the ears of corn. She ran her fingers over the stalks and broke off an ear, and then another. As she reached out to grab another one, a gunshot exploded in the air. Flocks of birds flew into the sky all around her. Another shot followed, and she began to run.

"Thieves, get out of my fields!" a man yelled.

Juana couldn't see where she was going. Another shot followed so close to her its deafening noise left her ears ringing.

She fell to the ground, the ears of corn rolled away from her. She scrambled to her feet and continued running through the cornstalks and felt the knifelike leaves slicing the skin of her legs and arms.

Juana ran across the dead tree over the river and didn't stop running until she was home. She panted for air and stood outside looking at her hands. They were empty.

Don Elías showed up the next day with two judiciales dressed in black uniforms and caps. Juana tried to close the door on them but one of the judiciales pushed the door back open.

"Where's your mother?" Don Elías asked.

Juana turned to look at her mother, who was lying on the cot. Amá's face was pale, and she had lavender circles under her eyes. She hadn't been sleeping well. Her stomach couldn't hold anything down, and her legs were now too weak to support her.

Before Juana could answer, Don Elías and the police officers pushed her aside and went into the shack. Amá's eyes widened with fear.

"I told you, Lupe, that the next time I wouldn't be nice," Don Elías said.

"Señora García, failure to repay a debt is a serious crime. And Don Elías here has pressed charges against you for theft," one of the judiciales said.

"We must take you down to the station," the other said.

Juana ran to the cot and stood between them and her mother. "Get out of our house. I won't let you take my mother away. Get out!"

The judiciales removed the rifles they carried on their backs and placed them in front of them.

Amá put her hands up. "Please, there's no need for that." She put an arm around Juana and then looked at Don Elías. "Please, señor, be merciful. I cannot go to prison. My daughter, señor, I cannot leave my daughter."

"Lupe, I have offered to help you repay your debt," Don Elías said as he walked up to her. "It didn't need to come to this."

"Please, señor," Amá said.

"We can work things out, I'm sure. We can make other arrangements," Don Elías said. "Can't we?"

Juana looked at Amá. She didn't know what to think. What kind of arrangements did he mean? She didn't want to lose her mother, but could she bear to see her mother put her pride aside and make "arrangements" with that man?

Amá looked at Juana. "Please let me speak to my daughter in private," she said to Don Elías.

The judiciales looked at Don Elías. When he nodded the three of them went outside. Amá rested her hands on Juana's shoulders and gently pushed her down on the cot. She remained standing.

"My daughter," she said. "I do not know why our prayers have not been answered. It is as if La Virgencita cannot hear us anymore. She's deaf to our pleas. And now it has come to this. I know the decision I have made will condemn me, yet I do not see another way. But know this. I love your father still, Juana. I will always love your father."

"Amá, what—?"

"Hush, mi'ja. Just know that I'm always going to be with you. I was made an orphan when I was very little. I know how painful it is not to have a mother to love you and care for you. I will not put you through that."

Amá kissed Juana on her forehead and then went outside. Juana didn't hear what Amá said to Don Elías. All she knew was that Don Elías left with a smile, saying he would return tomorrow to collect his first payment.

Amá sent Juana to play with the kids down at the vacant lot by Don Agustín's house. Juana didn't feel like going, but she knew Amá wanted to be alone.

Down at the vacant lot, the boys were finishing a soccer game. They were laughing, yelling, congratulating each other on good plays. Juana was a good player and wanted to play soccer with the boys, but they never let girls on the team. Her father had often played with her outside the shack, even though her mother never really approved. Amá had always wanted to give Apá a little son to play soccer with.

"Hey, Juana, I heard Don Elías has his eye on your mother."

Juana looked at the girls playing jump rope. One of them was standing to the side, waiting her turn. It was she who had spoken up.

"Well, that's not true. And why don't you mind your own business?" Juana said.

"Well, I heard your father has forgotten you and your mother," another girl said. "He probably already found himself a gringa."

The girls giggled.

"You shut up!" Juana said. "You don't know anything about my father. So just shut up! Shut up!"

Juana bent down and picked up some pebbles from the

ground. She threw them at the girls, and when her hands were empty, she took off running down to the river. Her tears didn't let her see clearly where she was going, but she could hear the rushing of the water up ahead. When she got there she stood under one of the guamúchil trees growing alongside the bank and looked down at the water.

The wind rustled the leaves of the trees, and the current rushed past her, going to places she'd never been to. She slowly got into the cold water. Her dress expanded like an umbrella and floated around her.

Since she didn't know how to swim, her toes instantly dug into the mud, trying to anchor her body and keep her from being carried away by the current. She sat on one of the flat washing stones. She and Amá sometimes came down to the river to wash their clothes. She remembered that the river snaked around to the other side of the mountains. Could it take her there, to the other side, to find Apá?

"Juana, what are you doing?"

She turned around and saw her godmother standing behind her, holding on to her little daughter, Sara.

"I'm just thinking," Juana said.

"Get out of the river, Juana, you can't swim. You don't want to cause more grief to your mother. I don't think she could bear to lose another child."

Juana lowered her head. Amá had already lost one child because of her.

"I'm sorry, Juana, I didn't mean to say such things. Forgive me, but I'm just worried about Lupe. Come, give me your hand."

Juana reached out and grabbed Antonia's hand. She

walked alongside her, heading to her shack. Sara darted into the bushes to chase the fireflies.

"I've tried to borrow money, Juana, but I've only managed to get about forty pesos," Antonia said.

Juana didn't say anything. She didn't want to tell Antonia what had happened with Don Elías. She didn't want to tell her it was now useless to try to borrow money from people.

"I got one!" Sara caught a firefly and held it inside her cupped hands. She peeked through the gaps between her fingers to look at it. "Look, Juana, look!" she said as she ran to her. "If we catch a lot of them we could light up your whole house. You can pretend you have electricity!"

Juana forced Sara's hands open and let the firefly out. "No, Sara. They have to be free, or else they die."

Don Elías showed up smelling like he'd just put on a whole bottle of cologne. Juana fought hard not to cover her nose when she opened the door. He was smiling, and in his hand he held a fresh bouquet of red roses.

He cleared his throat and then asked for Amá.

Juana glanced at her mother. She was sitting motionless on the cot. The whole morning she'd been sitting there, not saying a word. But last night, she had cried until the early hours of dawn. When the light of day started streaming in through the cracks between the bamboo sticks, Amá had wiped her last tear away.

"Is he here?" Amá finally turned around and looked at her. Juana nodded.

"Good afternoon, Lupe!" Don Elías called out, smiling. Amá came to the door and looked at Don Elías, who was freshly showered but still smelling of sweat, despite the cologne. She didn't say anything to him. Instead, she looked at Juana and asked her to leave.

"But Amá—"

"Go, Juana. Go to Antonia's house. She's invited you over for lunch. I told her you would go."

Juana looked down at her bare feet. She couldn't leave Amá alone with that man. She just couldn't.

"Juana, please," Amá said. "You must do as I tell you."

Don Elías cleared his throat and looked impatiently at Juana. She looked at her mother one last time before heading out the door. She started walking down to the river, not really knowing what to do. She turned around and saw Amá still standing there, watching her leave. Was she waiting to make sure she left?

Juana kept walking, but once in a while she would glance back at the shack. Finally, the door to the shack was closed. She bent down to pick a dandelion tickling her foot. "Apá, please write to us," she said to the wind flapping her hair. She looked at the mountains and blew on the dandelion, watching her words being carried away on the puffy seeds, like miniature parachutes floating in the wind.

Juana turned around to look back at her shack. Amá said her godmother was waiting for her for lunch, but she didn't feel like eating. How could she eat anything knowing Don Elías and Amá were alone? And what if he harmed her?

She ran back to the shack and stopped at the door, panting for air. When she caught her breath she tried to push the door in, but the door didn't budge. It was locked from the inside.

Juana walked around to the side of the shack and put her face against the wall. Through the cracks between the bamboo sticks she saw something that made her eyes widen with disgust.

She saw her mother naked, bending over the cot. And behind her, and just as naked as she, was Don Elías, grunting and puffing as he pushed against her.

Sometimes when Juana went to visit Doña Martina, she would help her feed the pigs she had in her pen. Once, when she was on her way to feed them, she heard one of the pigs squealing so loudly it hurt her ears. She ran to it, thinking something was wrong. When she got there she saw a male pig on top of a squealing sow. The sow was trying to get him off her, but the male held on, refusing to let go. The sow squealed as loudly as she could, but it could not escape the rape.

"Make him stop, Doña Martina. Make him stop!" Juana had yelled.

Doña Martina had put her arm around Juana and said, "Don't worry, Juana, they are making love. Soon we will have piglets. And I will give you one."

But when the piglets were born, the mother pig killed them all.

Juana watched her mother's face contorting in pain. Amá wasn't screaming, she wasn't groaning, she wasn't making any noise. But Juana covered her ears and imagined the squealing of a sow being raped.

Juana came back home in the evening. She entered the dark shack, wondering where her mother was. Neither the candles on the altar nor the candles on the table were lit. Juana made her way to the table and set down the pot of soup Antonia had given her to bring to Amá. She struck a match and lit a candle, watching the flame dance in front of her, flickering orange, red, yellow, and a little bit of blue on the tip.

She looked around, at the strange shadows the candlelight cast on the bamboo walls. And then she saw Amá, huddled against the corner, her long, black hair draped over her like a shawl. Around her were all her plates and cups.

"Amá?" Juana said. She walked over to her mother and tried to lift her up.

"Don't touch me, Juana," Amá said. "I'm not clean."

"Get up from the floor, Amá, come eat something."

Amá shook her head. She wrapped her arms around her legs, hid her face within her hair, and began to rock herself back and forth, back and forth. Juana decided to leave her there, and instead began to pick up the plates.

"Leave them there, Juana," Amá said.

Juana kept putting the plates in the box, being careful not to break them.

"I said leave them there!" Amá yanked a plate from Juana. She held the plate in front of her and said, "Why?" She shook the plate over and over.

Juana tried to take the plate from Amá. Amá snatched the plate from her, threw it into the box along with the rest of the plates, and then ran outside with the box. Juana ran after her.

"Amá, give them back. Give them back!"

Outside, Amá started throwing the plates against the rocks. One by one the plates went flying, crashing into a hundred pieces.

"How could you do this to me? How?" Amá yelled before she sent a cup flying.

Juana ran to stop her mother, but Amá pushed her away and continued throwing cups, saucers, and plates. Juana grabbed the last plate from Amá. She pulled and pulled, Amá refused to let it go.

"Give it to me. Give it to me," Amá said. But Juana dug her heels into the ground and pulled harder. Finally, she stood in front of her mother holding on to the last plate, the only plate left of her inheritance.

adelina

Adelina stared at the young man as he walked down the aisle to the restroom. What was it about him that made her body ache with pain? He turned to look briefly at her. She wanted to close her eyes. There was something in the tilt of his head, the crooked nose, and the droopy eyes that made her heart feel as if an invisible hand was squeezing it tight.

She turned to look out the window as the bus pulled off the highway to unload a few passengers. She was two hours away from her destination. An Indian woman standing outside the bus held her hand out for alms. She had a small boy strapped to her back with a rebozo. She slowly walked alongside the bus with her hand extended. Passengers looked the other way, pretending not to see her.

Adelina heard the restroom door open but didn't turn to look at the young man heading to his seat. Instead, she hugged the box that contained her father's ashes closer to her chest.

There was a tap on her window, and Adelina turned to see

the woman holding her hand up. Adelina looked at the boy and saw the mucus running down his nose. The bus began to move forward. The woman quickened her steps. Adelina quickly took out two twenty-dollar bills and handed them to the woman. She hadn't yet exchanged her dollars for pesos.

"Para su hijo," she said. For your son. The woman pressed the bills to her mouth and waved to Adelina as the bus pulled back onto the highway. Adelina looked at the woman through the cloud of dust the bus left behind in its wake.

juana

From the rock at the very top of the hill, Juana could see the town below, the towers of the church sticking out like two fingers pointing at the sky, the fields, the river that divided them in half, the mountains encircling the town. But it was the mountains to the west that most held her attention. Those were the mountains Apá had pointed at and said he would be on the other side of.

Juana watched the moon beginning to inch its way across the sky. Over the course of the month, it had changed from being a sliver to what it was now, almost a complete circle, bright and full.

This was how Amá had changed, too. Little by little. The wind blew the words of the townspeople's talk through the streets, and reached Juana and Amá.

"There goes Don Elías's puta," they said.

"I can't imagine what Miguel would say if he came back and found his wife in that condition, in the arms of another man."

"Ni Dios lo quiera."

It had been nine months since Apá left, seven and a half since Don Elías started coming to the shack every day. And Amá was now a full moon. A rounded belly. A baby growing inside her.

Don Elías walked around town with his chest puffed up like a rooster's. Juana wondered why his wife had never borne him a child. And she also wondered why the rest of the women who had fallen prey to Don Elías had never gotten pregnant either. Why did it have to be her mother?

Many months ago, Amá had stopped tending her altar. No candles were lit at night, no prayers were said. The flowers were no longer replaced with fresh wildflowers. They had withered long ago, and now only the stalks remained in the vases, the dry petals scattered on the altar like confetti.

Amá's black rosary lay untouched on the table. The statues of the saints and La Virgen de Guadalupe had been turned around to face the wall.

"The saints have all gone deaf," Amá had told Juana.

Juana wished she had the courage to turn them around. But she couldn't bring herself to do it. They would see the things Amá did not want them to see.

In the middle of the night Juana woke up and tiptoed to the door. She was going up to her rock to watch the full moon. She unlocked the door and slowly opened it, trying to make no noise.

"Where are you going, Juana?"

Juana turned around to look into the darkness, but she couldn't see Amá in the cot where she lay. Amá no longer slept with her. In a way Juana was glad. She didn't want to sleep with her mother anymore, knowing Don Elías's baby was inside her.

"I'm going to the outhouse to pee," Juana lied.

"Auggghhh!"

Juana took a step toward Amá. What was wrong with her? "Amá?"

"The baby's coming, Juana. Run down to Don Agustín's house and tell Doña Martina to come."

Juana ran to the cluster of shacks farther down the river.

She knocked on the door. "Doña Martina? Doña Martina?" She looked up at the moon. She was right. The moon was full tonight.

"Who is it?" Don Agustín asked from inside the shack.

"It's Juana. The baby's coming."

Doña Martina opened the door. "It is time?"

Juana nodded.

They made their way back to the shack. When they got there, Juana lit the candles on the table. She took all the dusty candles from the altar and put them on the floor around Amá's cot so Doña Martina could see better.

Amá was lying on the cot, taking small breaths to calm herself. Her face was bathed in perspiration.

"The water has broken," Amá said.

Doña Martina nodded. She put her hands on Amá's swollen stomach. "The baby is turned. It should not be a difficult birth."

Juana sat on her cot and looked toward Amá's cot surrounded by candles. The shadows of the flames danced on the walls. She watched Doña Martina light the coals in the brazier and put a pot of water to boil. She took out clean towels from her bag and put them on the table. Then she filled a bowl with water, sat next to Amá, and gently washed her face.

Juana wished she could help, that it was she washing the sweat from Amá's face, but she couldn't bring herself to stand up.

They spent the rest of the night listening to Amá's moans. By dawn, the contractions were close enough for Doña Martina to say it was time to push.

"Come help your mother, Juana," Doña Martina said. Juana reluctantly came to place pillows behind Amá and to help Doña Martina bend her mother's knees and scoot her feet closer to her thighs. Amá grabbed her knees and held on to them.

"Okay, Lupe, when you feel the contractions coming push as hard as you can," Doña Martina said.

Amá screamed as she pushed. She screamed and pushed. She screamed and pushed more. Juana felt pain, too—this was the first time she was witnessing a birth. She had not been present when María and Anita were born. Antonia had been the one to help Amá. But Antonia stopped coming around the day she noticed the latest bulge under Amá's dress.

"I can see the head, Lupe, keep pushing. It's almost out. You're almost there."

Amá let out a long scream. Doña Martina caught the baby on a towel and put her finger inside its mouth to clean it. The baby let out a cry. It sounded to Juana like the cry of a kitten.

"It's a boy, Lupe. It's a beautiful, healthy boy." Doña Martina put the baby on Amá's bare stomach, which was mapped with purple stretch marks. Juana watched the umbilical cord pulsing.

"A boy, a little boy," Amá said, crying. "My son."

Juana looked down at the baby. Her brother. The boy Amá had always wanted to give Apá.

The son Don Elías had wished for, and now had.

Doña Martina cleaned Amá, yet the blood kept coming.

"What's wrong with her?" Juana asked.

"She is badly torn," Doña Martina whispered so Amá wouldn't hear. "Juana, quick, find as many clean rags and towels as you can."

Juana did as she was told. Doña Martina took herbs from her bag and began to make a poultice.

"What's going on?" Amá asked, frightened. Juana watched the rags between her mother's legs quickly turn red. She replaced those rags with new ones.

"It's okay, Lupe, I'll take care of it. Don't worry. I'll take care of it," Doña Martina said.

"Martina, I feel cold. I feel so cold," Amá said. Juana rushed over to her cot and yanked the blanket from it. She shook it to make sure there were no scorpions hidden in the folds, then she ran back to her mother and put the blanket over her and the baby.

"I don't want to die, Juana. I don't want to die. The baby needs me. You need me, Juana . . ." Amá said.

"Shhh, Amá, everything's going to be fine. Everything's going to be fine." Juana leaned against her mother and wrapped her arms around her.

"Juana, keep your mother awake," Doña Martina said. "Don't let her fall asleep. Keep her awake."

Don Elías came bringing dozens of roses with him. He placed the bouquets on the floor by Amá's bed. Juana noticed that Amá tightened her hold on the baby, who was now nursing from her breast. Amá threw a blanket over the baby and herself to cover her exposed breast.

Juana wondered who had told him about the baby's birth yesterday. Surely it couldn't have been Doña Martina. She had only been gone for a few hours having labored hard to stop the hemorrhage. And even after she had finally made it stop, she did not rest. She stayed by Amá's side and checked her breathing while Amá slept. She bathed the baby with a sponge and dressed it with the clothes Amá had knitted over the past months.

Doña Martina left at noon, saying she would be back to check on Amá.

"My son, let me see my son," Don Elías said. Amá clutched the baby tighter.

"He's eating," she said. Don Elías seemed to have not heard her. He pulled the blanket off Amá to gaze down at the baby. Juana looked at her mother's bare breast. She wanted to run to the cot and cover her. Don Elías leaned closer to the baby. Amá looked away, and Juana could see tears gathering in her eyes.

"You have to leave," Amá said. "The baby needs to sleep."

"Now, Lupe, I'm not going to go anywhere. I want to see my son. I want to hold him," Don Elías said. "You can't deny me that."

"My mother needs to rest," Juana said. Was the man daft? Why couldn't he understand that Amá was tired and weak from losing so much blood?

"Stay out of this, girl," Don Elías said. "If it wasn't for this baby, you would have starved a long time ago."

Juana looked at her mother. What did he mean by that? Amá looked away, ashamed.

"What, didn't your mother tell you where all the food she brought came from?" Don Elías asked.

"That's enough, Elías," Amá said.

"You took money from him, didn't you?" Juana asked. "Everything you brought home was not given to you by Doña Martina or my godmother, it came from him!" Juana said, pointing at Don Elías. She wished she could vomit all the food she had eaten in the last seven months.

"Juana," Amá said, "I had no other choice. I had to think about you. I had to think about the baby. If I didn't eat well he would have been affected by it, don't you understand?"

"Yes, my son," Don Elías said, again. "He will be my heir. He will be my pride. I'm going to raise him into a—"

"You'll do no such thing," Amá said. "*I* am going to raise him into a good man. I'm going to take care of him and teach him the values a man must have. Respect, honesty, and above all, compassion."

Don Elías cleared his throat. The baby let go of Amá's

breast, sound asleep. Amá tucked her breast back into her dress.

"Now, Lupe, you can't keep me out of my son's life. I'm his father, don't forget that." He took the baby from Amá's arms and cradled him. The baby stirred in his sleep and began to cry. Juana watched Don Elías hold the baby. She felt like snatching the baby from him.

"He's a big boy, isn't he, Lupe?" Don Elías asked. "Imagine if he had been born at nine months, instead of seven and a half?"

Juana looked at the baby.

"Don't say nonsense," Amá said. "The boy's not big."

Don Elías got drunk that night and told everyone he ran into about his new baby boy. The next morning, as Juana walked down the street to catch the bus to the mercado to buy chicken feet and vegetables for a stew, she could hear everyone talk about it. El descaro de Lupe. Did she have no shame giving birth to a son who was not her husband's child? And that's not all. How dare she have a son with a married man? A man whose wife had not been able to bear her own children.

While she waited for the bus, Juana kept looking at the ground, thinking about Amá and the baby. She promised herself she would look for a job first thing in the morning. She was almost thirteen years old. Soon she would be a young woman.

She sensed someone looking at her. Two eyes whose gaze was burning into her. Juana looked up and saw a row of taxicabs in front of her, waiting for the traffic to move. She looked at the passenger in one of the cabs. Don Elías's wife stared out the cab window at Juana. She was so close that Juana could clearly see the woman's eyes, red and swollen, as if her eyes had been stung by bees.

adelina

"Adelina? Dr. Luna is here," Maggie said. "He'd like to visit with Laura for a little bit, see how she's doing."

Adelina turned around and saw him standing next to Maggie. He was dressed in jeans and a long-sleeve blue shirt. His hair was neatly combed back. Her breath caught in her throat. He was smiling at her the way she imagined a young schoolboy would smile at the girl he likes, timid and sweet.

She felt herself blushing.

"Yes, of course. Come in, Dr. Luna," she said.

"Good afternoon, Dr. Luna," Laura said as she sat up in bed. "It's nice of you to come visit me."

Adelina closed the book she'd been reading to Laura and stood to go.

"You're welcome to stay," Dr. Luna said. "I'll only be a few minutes. I don't want to interrupt your reading."

Adelina put the book down on the nightstand and looked at his green eyes. She needed to put some distance between herself and those eyes. It scared her the way his presence made her feel. She wouldn't let this man come into her life, not after she had worked so hard to put herself back together. She didn't want any man in her life. She'd had enough. The only man she'd allowed to stay in her heart was her father. Even if he was only a memory.

"You may stay as long as you wish, Doctor," Adelina said. "If you'll excuse me, I'll leave you two to talk." She walked out of the room, her heart pounding. She had wanted to stay, but she couldn't bring herself to do it.

juana

The next time Don Elías came to the shack, his wife came with him. As soon as Juana saw her standing behind him, she tried to slam the door shut. Her heart started beating fast. Why would Doña Matilde be here with her husband?

"Move aside, girl," Don Elías said. He pushed Juana to the side and he and his wife walked into the shack. Amá was rocking the baby in her arms, singing a lullaby. She stopped singing when she saw them come in and pressed the baby closer to her.

"What do you want?"

"Listen, Lupe, my wife here—" Don Elías began.

"I want the baby," Doña Matilde said.

"What?" Amá and Juana said at the same time.

"I said, I want the baby, and I'm taking him with me," Doña Matilde repeated.

Amá struggled to get up, but her body was still too weak from the hemorrhage. Doña Martina said she would have to stay in bed for a while, until she healed. Amá winced in pain but was still able to lower her feet down. Juana ran to her mother and tried to get her to lie down again.

Amá shook her head and asked her to move aside.

"I don't know what evil game you are playing, señora," Amá said to Doña Matilde. "But this is my son, and no one is going to take him from me."

"Lupe, be reasonable," Don Elías said. "Look at where you live. You have no money. You have nothing. You can't take care of my son. I will give him everything. Everything."

Amá kept shaking her head. "I said you're not taking him from me!"

"I am," Doña Matilde said as she came to stand in front of Amá. Juana could see the white in her eyes covered by tiny red veins. Her eyes were still puffy from crying. "Do you think, señora," she said, "that you could sleep with my husband, that you could take his love from me, that you could give him a child, and that I would allow it? Did you honestly think you could leave me with nothing and that I was going to stand aside and let you?"

Amá clutched the baby even tighter. She hid her face into the hollow of his neck. The baby began to whimper, having been pulled out of his sleep by all the angry voices.

"Shhhhh, Miguelito, shhhhhh," Amá said.

"Miguelito? How dare you name him after that imbecile who abandoned you?" Don Elías roared.

Juana looked at Amá, herself surprised that Amá had actually given the baby Apá's name.

"If I dared to name my son after my husband, it is because this baby is his!" Amá yelled. She held out the crying baby to

Don Elías. "Do you see him? Do you? He's not your son. He is Miguel's son."

Juana could not believe what she was hearing. Apá's son. Her brother. Her full-blooded brother.

"You lying bitch!" Don Elías said. He reached out and slapped Amá.

"Stop making up lies," Doña Matilde said. "I'm taking this baby whether you agree or not. I'm entitled to him. I'm the wife. I'm the one who should've had this baby."

Her hands suddenly darted out and yanked the baby from Amá. Amá was startled for a moment, but soon threw herself upon Doña Matilde and tried to get the baby back. Juana threw herself upon Doña Matilde, too. The baby's cries were now deafening.

Don Elías lifted Juana up and threw her onto the floor, then he grabbed Amá and pushed her onto the cot. Juana scrambled to stand up, but she had landed on her ankle. The pain shot up her leg as soon as she leaned her weight on it. She fell down to the floor again. She dragged herself to Amá and noticed a thin streak of blood running down her mother's leg.

Amá limped toward Doña Matilde, unaware of the blood. "Give me back my son. P-lea-se give him to me." She reached out to grab the baby, but Doña Matilde and Don Elías were already heading toward the door. Amá dropped onto the floor and began to drag herself toward them. Juana grabbed hold of the cot and raised herself up. On one foot, she started hopping toward Don Elías.

"Give us back the baby!" she yelled. "Give him back!"

"Stay away from me, stay away from my wife, and stay

away from my son," Don Elías said to Amá, "or I'll have you thrown in jail for the rest of your life."

Don Elías ushered his wife out the door. Amá dragged herself to the threshold. Juana limped behind her. From there, both of them could see Don Elías and his wife walking away, taking the baby with them.

Juana looked down at her mother lying on the floor. Her dress was stained with blood. Her face was bathed in mucus and tears. Juana pressed her hand against her chest. She felt a deep, deep hatred begin to swell inside of her, like a balloon filling with water.

adelina

Adelina glanced at the campesino riding atop his donkey. He wore a straw hat to shield him from the sun. The bus passed by him so quickly, she didn't even get a chance to get a good look at him, but she'd caught a glimpse of the machete dangling at his side. Was he on his way to the fields?

Upon seeing him, the reality of the situation hit her. She was back in Mexico, on her way to see her mother who was lying on her deathbed.

She got the phone call a week ago. She'd not picked up the phone at first, wondering if it was Sebastian. She let the answering machine pick up. A part of her wished he'd persisted, but she knew she had finally driven him away.

"It's your mother," the voice on the machine said. "She has fallen ill, and the doctor doesn't think she'll make it much longer. Give me a call when you get this message, I'll—"

Adelina rushed to the phone and picked it up. "Sandra, it's me. What's wrong with my mother?"

Adelina closed her eyes, trying to picture the woman on the other end of the line. She'd only seen her a few times. But throughout the years, she'd been the only link to her past.

"Your mother's very ill, and the doctor doesn't think she'll make it. She's been asking for you. And in her sleep she calls out to your father, asking him when he's going to come home."

"How long does she have?"

"I don't know. She's old now, and being locked up like that doesn't help. Besides, she's stopped eating, too. The doctor says that's the reason why her body can't fight off the infection. She's too weak. It's as if she's willing herself to die."

"Tell her I'm coming home to her," Adelina said softly, feeling a cold pit in her stomach. She couldn't believe she was saying that. "And I'll bring my father back to her. Even if it's the last thing I do. I will bring him home to her."

"God be with you, mi'ja," the woman said.

Even when the line went dead, Adelina kept the phone receiver pressed against her ear.

She felt a deep pain swelling inside her body. As if that phone call had removed the scab that had grown over a deep cut.

juana

Juana stood in the doorway and felt the rain splashing on her bare feet. She wrapped her mother's rebozo tight around her and peered through the darkness, wondering where her mother was. She leaned against the door frame and took a deep breath. The summer rains had come again. She looked at the puddle of water at her feet, and saw how little by little the water was creeping into the shack. She hoped the river would not flood this year.

The rain sounded like the click-clacking of a horse's hooves on the roof. The sound became louder, and when Juana saw the silhouette of a horse and rider through the rain she realized it was the horse, not the rain, making the sound. She watched as the horse got closer and closer. She couldn't see the rider, for a poncho covered him, and he wore a sombrero on his head. She wrapped the rebozo tighter around her and waited. Could it be her father? Was he finally back? She ran to the table and grabbed the candle, and then went back to the door.

The horse stopped in front of her. She raised the candle,

cupping her hand over the flame to protect it from the rain. The man tilted his head down and looked at her. She caught a glimpse of the silver mustache before the rain drops extinguished the flame of the candle.

"Buenas noches, Juana."

"Good evening, señor, how can I help you?" Juana looked at the old man's face, struggling to hide her disappointment.

"Your mother needs your help, child. She's down at the cemetery, calling out to her children as if she were La Llorona."

Juana now recognized the man. It was Don José, the night watchman. "I don't understand. My mother wouldn't—"

"She's drunk."

She thought about the empty beer bottles her mother had been hiding under the bed. Amá promised she would stop drinking, but now Juana realized it was only getting worse.

"She's at the foot of your sister's grave, ranting and raving like a loca. I tried to calm her down, but she lashed at me with a broken tequila bottle. You must come and see if you can talk some sense into her. Perhaps she has calmed down."

Juana nodded and took his hand. Don José lifted her up and put her in front of him. Juana felt the rain sting her eyes and put the rebozo over her head.

Juana dismounted the horse in front of her sister's grave. She saw her mother sitting beside the wooden cross, soaking wet.

"Amá?" Juana slowly approached her mother. "Amá?"

"Leave me alone, Juana," Amá said.

"Amá, we need to go home. You need to get out of the rain. You may catch a chill."

"And what does it matter if I live or die?"

"It matters to me. Come Amá, let's go home." Juana put her hands on her mother's shoulders and tried to help her up. Amá pushed her away.

"Get away from me!"

"But Amá—"

"Let me be. I'm praying to my dead daughters. I'm asking them for help. They are angelitos in Heaven. They can intercede for me and ask God to help me, to listen to my pleas."

"Señora, listen to your daughter. It's late, and you should go home and rest," Don José said.

Amá pointed at Anita's grave. "Look at that, look at that rain falling over my Anita. She must be cold and lonely. She was just a baby, just a little baby. "

Juana squatted beside her mother. "Let's go home, Amá."

"She would've been two years old now. She would've been walking already, saying a few words. But I'll never get to see her again. I lost her. And now I have lost my son as well."

"Amá, we'll get him back. We will."

Amá shook her head. "If Anita was still alive, none of this would've happened. Miguel wouldn't have left. And I would still have my son by my side." Amá suddenly turned to her. Juana wiped the rain from her eyes and looked at her mother's face streaked with mud.

"Why did you fall asleep?"

Juana looked down at the ground. Her body trembled, and she tried hard to keep it still.

Amá seized her by her shoulders. "Why did you fall asleep, Juana? I told you to take care of her. I told you."

Juana bit her lips. Amá grabbed her head and forced her to look at the muddy grave. "Say something to your sister. Say something."

Don José got off his horse and walked toward them, "Señora, calm down."

Amá pushed her down on the grave. Juana didn't struggle. She felt the mud inside her mouth, felt the rain splashing in her eyes, felt her hair twisted around her mother's fingers.

"Say something! Say something, damn you!"

"Lupe, let her go."

"Say something!"

Juana dug her fingers into the mud, lifted her head, and screamed.

adelina

Diana wasn't in her bed. Adelina walked quietly around the room, looking at the five other women sleeping soundly in their beds. Only Diana's bed was empty.

"I'm right here."

Adelina turned around. She had distinctly heard Diana's voice. She turned to the windows and saw a hand pull the curtain aside.

"You scared me," Adelina said.

Diana said nothing. She turned to look back at the moon and leaned her forehead on the windowpane.

"Can't sleep?" Adelina asked.

"I don't want to sleep," she said. "I never want to sleep again."

Adelina noticed the silvery haze the moonlight cast on Diana's face. She heard Diana shiver. "You should rest, Diana. Come to bed and warm yourself with your blankets. It's a cold night tonight."

Diana stayed where she was. "I want to look at the moon," she said. Her eyes became glazed with tears.

"That was the last thing I remember," Diana said. "I remember I was looking at the moon, thinking about how late it was and wishing we were already home. Then I closed my eyes for a second, only for a second, and when I opened them the car was already heading down the hill, bumping over rocks and crashing into bushes, and when it flipped over I could see the moon spinning around and around. . . ." Diana covered her face with her hands and sobbed.

Adelina put her hand on Diana's shoulder and wished she could say the right words to make the pain go away, but she knew that nothing she said would ease Diana's suffering. "We're all here for you, Diana. You're not alone. I understand—"

Diana pushed Adelina's hand away. "What do you understand? You don't know what it's like, to live with this guilt. I killed my son. Do you understand that? I fell asleep driving and killed my son. I killed my son!"

Adelina pulled Diana against her chest and held her while she sobbed. In the eight days she'd been at the shelter, Diana had not told anyone, not even the counselors, this had happened to her. Now Adelina understood Diana's silence, and her addiction to alcohol.

"Why did I fall asleep? Why?"

"We're going to help you through this, Diana, I promise," Adelina said.

"You don't know what it's like," Diana said. "You don't . . ."

juana

Juana had walked Amá home from the cemetery and put her in her cot. As soon as Amá fell asleep, Juana filled her father's canteen and headed toward the mountains. She had now been walking since dawn, stopping once in a while to drink water and catch her breath. The sun was directly in front of her. In a few hours, it would start its descent into the mountains up ahead.

The sky was clear, except for a few puffy clouds being pushed about by the wind. The sun beat on Juana's face, and she raised her hand up to shield her eyes. She felt as if she was leaning into flames, just like bakers did when they put bread inside the oven to bake. But she was grateful for the heat. The sun had long ago dried her wet clothes, and its heat made the chill that seized her body more bearable. She should have brought more water. The canteen she carried inside her back-pack was almost empty, and the river was far away from her now. How far had she walked? The mountains looked just as small as when she had first started. She wasn't getting any closer.

But on the other side of those mountains, she would find Apá. And when she found him she would not be angry at him. She would not yell at him for forgetting about them. She would not cry and beat her fists against his chest, demanding explanations. She would only ask him one thing. Do you still love us, Apá? And if he answered yes, then she would tell him all about his son, the baby Don Elías stole from them almost three months ago. But she would not tell him about Amá, and about the empty beer bottles under the bed. This, she would not tell him.

Juana stopped to catch her breath. She looked at the wet ground steaming under the heat of the sun and at the bushes and cacti around. She had left the fields long ago. From where she stood, she could see the corn growing in straight lines.

In a few days it would be her thirteenth birthday, and she had already made her birthday wish, which was to find her father and to convince him to come home.

If he came back, he could go to the police station and press charges against Don Elías. They would listen to him, for no one had listened to her and Amá. Don Elías would have to return the baby. If he came back, Amá would have a baby to nurse, instead of a beer bottle every night. And she would stop squeezing her breasts, crying because they were now dry. And if he came back, perhaps Amá would forgive her for Anita's death.

The mountains weren't getting any closer. Or was it just her imagination? Surely last night, just before everything was plunged into darkness after the sun had set, the mountains had seemed a bit closer. But now, in the early hours of the morning, they seemed to be far away.

Juana tilted the empty canteen and rolled her tongue inside it, trying to lick any leftover drops. But there were none. She walked and walked, her eyes focused on the mountains in front of her. She didn't even bother to remove the pebble she had in her shoe. She let it hurt her. At least the pain in her heel would keep her from thinking about the hunger pains in her stomach, or the pain in her dry throat, or the shivers that made her body tremble.

She stopped to catch her breath and leaned against a rock. The wind whipped her face with her hair. Rain clouds were gathering above her. She would welcome the rain. She needed water. There was a small puddle of rainwater hidden under a rock, and she scooped up a little bit of water to wet her hot forehead and the nape of her neck. She let a few drops trickle down her throat before hugging her knees close to her chest as her body shivered.

When she opened her eyes, Juana didn't know where she was. She was inside a shack very similar to her own. But this shack smelled of almond oil and epazote. She could hear the soft cooing of doves. Doves everywhere.

Was she dead?

"She's burning up," a man said.

"I've tried to cure her," a woman said. "But it takes long to heal a broken heart."

"Yes, it will be a while."

"Now hush, let the girl rest."

• • •

Apá is standing behind Juana, squeezing lemons into a bucket of water. Juana is sitting on the lavadero, waiting for her bath.

"Will you tell me a story, Apá?" she asks. He nods and tells her the story of La Llorona, the weeping woman who, in a moment of desperation, took her children to the river and drowned them. "But you don't like the tale of La Llorona," she says.

He laughs, and laughs, and laughs. Suddenly, he throws a bucket of water on top of Juana. Cold lemon water that stings her eyes, and she screams.

"There, there, Juana." Doña Martina was putting wet clothes on Juana's forehead. She put a bottle of alcohol under Juana's nose and held it there for a few seconds, until the smell reached Juana's brain and the darkness went away.

She smiled at Juana, and for a moment her gap-toothed smile made her look like a little girl who had just lost her first tooth. But her eyes were sad, and the wrinkles around them made her look like an old woman again.

"The fever has broken," she said. "You must try hard to get better."

"How did you find me?" Juana asked.

"When I went to check on your mother, I didn't see you in the house. I asked her where you were, but she was too drunk to tell me anything. She just kept saying you left. That she had lost you, too. I sent my husband to look for you. He ran into some campesinos who said they'd seen a young girl earlier that day pass by the fields where they were working, heading toward the mountains."

Juana thought she could have made it. If she had brought more water, she would have made it.

"They found you at the foot of the mountains right before the rain started. You were burning up with fever."

Doña Martina lifted a cup of water for her to drink, except Juana turned her head away and wouldn't drink. She had failed. She had not found Apá.

"Juana, you need to be strong. Your mother needs you."

"She hates me."

"You need to give her time, Juana. Your mother has gone through so much. First, your father left and has sent no word. And now she has lost her child. It is too painful. She has lost so many children now."

Juana tried to swallow her tears. She wouldn't cry. She said she wouldn't. But she broke down.

"I couldn't make it," she said through the tears. "I couldn't make it. I couldn't make it."

"What are you talking about, Juana?"

"The mountains. I had to cross the mountains to find Apá."

"But your father is not on the other side of the mountains."

Juana looked up at Doña Martina.

"Niña, the United States is very, very far away."

"But Apá said he would be right around those mountains. And he told me to look at them whenever I needed him!"

Doña Martina was quiet for a moment. "Maybe he told you that so you wouldn't feel so bad about him leaving. Don't judge your father and think he was lying. He just didn't want to hurt you even more."

Juana looked at Doña Martina. Apá wasn't on the other side of the mountains. He wasn't close to her, after all.

Doña Martina went to her wardrobe and brought a map. She laid it on the bed, over Juana, and then showed her the state of Guerrero, where they lived. She ran her finger up, past the states of Michoacán, Jalisco, Nayarit, Sinaloa, Sonora, Baja California. . . . Then her finger crossed a thick black line and stopped moving. Juana looked at where Doña Martina's finger pointed. Little black letters the size of fleas jumped up at her. They spelled the words "Los Angeles." That was when Juana realized what Doña Martina said was true. Apá was not on the other side of these mountains. And in order to find him, she would have to cross not just these mountains, but perhaps a hundred more.

adelina

Don Ernesto had never married or fathered a child. He never asked Adelina much about her past. It was as if he understood her life had started the moment she got to Los Angeles.

All she told him about herself was that she was here to look for her father. He'd nodded in understanding and said he would help her find him.

"But what will you do in between that?" he'd asked.

"What do you mean?" she asked him, not really understanding what he meant.

"What I mean to say is that looking for your father is not exactly a career. You need to go to school, Adelina. You need to educate yourself, get a degree. That is, on your time off, when you're not searching for your father."

Adelina didn't know if he was mocking her or if he was serious. What did he mean about going to school, getting a degree?

"I'm sorry, child. You're dealing with an old schoolteacher.

I just hate to see a young woman like yourself do nothing with her life. I don't want you to be like other people who never tried to be somebody."

"I am here to find my father. Not to go to school. Not to get a degree. Not to be somebody. I'm fine being a nobody. But I want to be a nobody who found her father and took him home!" She slammed her fist down on the table.

"And if you don't find him, then what? One day you might find yourself an old woman, and like me, you'll still be living in this dump, with no family, and no one to love you."

Don Ernesto rested his hand on Adelina's shoulder. She instinctively moved away, and then became embarrassed for doing so. He excused himself and headed out of her room. He stopped in the doorway and said, "I know some men have hurt you, child. But don't forget that there are other men, such as your father, who care for you."

Adelina didn't have much luck finding her father. She obtained jobs in factories, hoping to find her father working in one of them. She would come home exhausted. Her feet hurt from standing the whole day. Her hands and arms hurt from ironing jeans or trimming thread ends. On the weekends she'd go to downtown L.A. and walk around, hoping to catch a glimpse of her father, but she never did.

Don Ernesto had asked the men living in the building to keep an eye out for Adelina's father. And before someone moved out of the building to go north to work in the fields, they would be told the same thing.

Finally, after six months of searching, Adelina let Don Ernesto take her to the local high school.

"But I don't know much about school, Don Ernesto," she told him.

"Don't worry, mi'ja. I will help you. And you will learn."

Adelina kissed Don Ernesto's wrinkled cheek before she let herself be guided down the hall to her first class.

juana

"So Doña Martina sent you?" Doña Josefina asked as she flipped the quesadillas over. Juana nodded, trying to keep her eyes on Doña Josefina. Her mouth had started to water when she glanced at the chicken quesadillas sizzling on the hot griddle.

"She cured my grandson once, you know," Doña Josefina said. "My daughter had no peace because the boy kept waking up crying at night, and during the day he just couldn't be still. Then Doña Martina came and did a cleaning. When she broke the egg open and put it in water we could see the shape of little eyes on the egg yolk. And you know what was wrong with him?"

"He had the evil eye," Juana answered, remembering the time Doña Martina did a cleaning for her sister María.

"You're a smart girl," Doña Josefina said. "And you look like a hard worker. I'll be happy to have you work for me."

Juana heard the shrill of the train whistle announcing its

departure. The people waiting on the benches scrambled to their feet and dragged their luggage toward the train.

She breathed a sigh of relief. "Thank you, señora."

For the rest of the day Juana made tortillas on the tortillera and burned her fingers once in a while trying to flip them over. Whenever the trains pulled into the station she would take a tray and walk from window to window, offering quesadillas to the passengers still on board. She tried to be quick on her feet, for there were other women selling food from other food stands as well. She especially tried to compete with the women working for Doña Rosa, the lady who had fired Amá because Don Elías told her to.

When the whistle blew Juana stepped away from the train and watched it pass by. Sometimes she waved at the passengers passing by her in a colorful blur.

"Hello, Tomás. I heard you're going back to El Otro Lado very soon." Doña Josefina waved at the man who had just finished purchasing tickets at the window. He came over to the food stand, waving his tickets in the air.

"You heard right, Josefina. In two days I'll go back to Los Angeles, and my son is coming with me."

Juana looked up from the quesadilla she was flipping. *He came from Los Angeles? Maybe he knows Apá!*

"Do you know my father?" she blurted.

"Your father?"

"He's living in Los Angeles. His name's Miguel García." She put a hand on her chest and breathed through her mouth, trying to slow down the beating of her heart.

"Miguel García, Doña Elena's son?"

Juana quickly nodded.

"I didn't know he was over there. I'm sorry, but I haven't seen him."

"Niña, you're burning my quesadillas!" Doña Josefina said.

Juana flipped the quesadillas on the griddle and burned herself. She put the burned finger inside her mouth and tried to flip them with her other hand. Her eyes became blurry with tears. She knew it wasn't because of the burn on her finger.

"Those quesadillas smell delicious," Don Tomás said. Juana turned to the table behind her and busied herself kneading dough. As she dug her fingers into it she remembered the times when she had made mud tortillas for Apá.

"Well, thank you very much, Josefina. I hope to see you again some other time when I come back."

"Está bién, Tomás. Say hello to Mayra for me. I'll make sure I visit her after you're gone. It'll be hard for her to see her husband and son leave."

Juana turned and watched him walk away, wondering how it was possible that he hadn't seen her father. Was Los Angeles very big? She wondered if she and Amá would be able to find him if they went to look for him.

"Excuse me, Doña Josefina!" Juana ran to catch up to Don Tomás. "Sir. Please, sir!"

Don Tomás turned to look at her.

"I-I was wondering if you could tell me how to get to El Otro Lado."

He chuckled and patted her shoulder with his train tickets.

"Why, are you thinking about going over there?" He laughed again.

Juana felt her cheeks getting hot. "N-no. I just want to know what my father's trip was like, t-that's all."

Don Tomás thought for a second and then said, "All right, I'll tell you. First, you catch the train to Cuernavaca and then take the bus to Mexico City, or you can take the bus directly from here to Mexico City. Then you transfer to another bus that will take you all the way to Tijuana. In about two days you'll get to the border. Then you need to find a coyote, and one way or another he'll take you to the other side."

"Is it hard?"

"It depends if you're lucky," he said. "I've done it three times already, and I've always made it just fine. It's a lot of walking, but walking never killed anyone." He patted her head and then disappeared behind the throng of people rushing to board the train.

Juana walked over to the ticket window and said, "Excuse me, how much does a ticket to Cuernavaca cost?"

When Juana got home, she saw her mother bending over something. When she got closer she noticed a large cardboard box that had been turned into some sort of lean-to, and lying inside it was a dog. A pregnant dog. Amá was feeding it tortillas soaked in water.

"What's going on?" Juana asked.

Again, Amá had not brushed her hair or changed her clothes. She'd been wearing the same dress for four days now. Juana couldn't remember the last time she had bathed.

"I found her wandering around the streets, with nowhere to

go," Amá said. "Look at her, poor thing, she's all bones now. And she's pregnant, Juana. She needs someone to take care of her." Amá's breath reeked of alcohol. Juana didn't want to tell her mother that it was difficult enough trying to find food for themselves. They couldn't afford having another mouth to feed. She looked down at the plate of quesadillas Doña Josefina had given her. At least tonight, they would have a good meal.

"Come, Amá, let's go down to the river to bathe ourselves and wash our clothes. Then we can come back and have a good dinner."

Amá shook her head. "No, no, no, Juana, I need to take care of Princesa. The puppies will be born any minute now." She looked at the plate Juana was holding. "What do you have in there?"

"I brought quesadillas. I got a job at the train station."

"Juana, you didn't ask Doña Rosa for a job, did you? Not after she fired me because of that hijo de la—"

"No, Amá, I work for someone else."

Suddenly, Amá swayed to the side. Juana tried to catch her. She hadn't realized Amá was that drunk.

"I'm okay," Amá said, steadying herself. She glanced at the plate Juana was holding. "Can we give some quesadillas to Princesa?"

"Of course not!" Juana said. "Let's go into the house to get the clothes ready. We need to go wash."

"But Juana, Princesa is pregnant. If she doesn't nourish herself the puppies—"

"Come, Amá, into the house. Princesa will be fine." Juana grabbed her mother's arm and gently ushered her inside.

• • •

For the hundredth time that week, Amá refused to go to the river and bathe. Juana finally managed to sit her mother down to have her hair brushed. She deftly twisted the strands of Amá's hair into a braid and tied it with a ribbon. She grabbed a rag, dipped it in water, and cleaned the dirt off her mother's face. She sprayed Amá with a little bit of her Avon perfume that smelled of jasmine.

Juana was soon looking at her beautiful mother again.

Amá looked at her for moment, and Juana noticed that her eyes were slightly swollen. She had been crying again.

"I saw him today," Amá said softly.

"Who?"

"Miguelito, my son."

"Amá, you need to stop going over there. If Don Elías sees you near his house he'll send you to jail."

"I had to see him, Juana. He's growing so quickly. Every day he looks more like your father."

Juana ran her hand over her mother's face. "One day we'll get him back, you'll see."

Amá covered her face and cried harder. Juana took out the pesos she'd put inside her brassiere. They were warm. It didn't matter how much she had to work; very soon, she and Amá would leave this place in search of her father. And then they would all return and claim Miguelito as their own.

adelina

Diana sliced her wrists with the lid of a can she'd found in the trash can. Adelina wasn't on duty at the time. She'd received a phone call from Jen, one of the social workers at the shelter. Adelina rushed to the hospital and waited for news about Diana. The doctor said she'd lost a lot of blood.

Sebastian wasn't the doctor who treated Diana that night. He had come to work early the next day. Adelina had been slouching in her chair while she waited outside in the waiting room. She was trying to fall asleep, but she'd forgotten her sleeping pills, and without them sleep would not come.

She sensed someone looking at her. When she opened her eyes she felt herself drowning in two green pools.

"Hello, Ms. Vasquez. Is something wrong?"

Adelina looked at the creases on his forehead and the tiny wrinkles at the corners of his eyes.

"It's Diana. She tried to kill herself." She rubbed her eyes. She knew they were red and swollen from crying. She'd been so afraid she would lose Diana.

Dr. Luna sat down next to her.

"I'm sorry to hear that. I'd hoped that going to counseling would help. But she seems to be carrying a heavy burden on her shoulders. Would you mind sharing her story with me?"

Adelina thought about this for a moment. She knew that by law, and by her code of honor, she was not to divulge any information about anyone living in the shelter. It was a violation of trust. Dr. Luna knew most of the women staying at the shelter, although he did not know their stories, and somehow she felt it would be all right to tell him. She wanted to tell him.

"She and her son were in a car accident a few years ago. It was late at night, and Diana fell asleep at the wheel. Her son died, and she lived."

"So now she feels guilty about surviving?" he asked.

She nodded. "Guilty and alone. He was the only family she had."

"And the loss of a child is extremely painful," Dr. Luna said.

Adelina looked at him, wondering if he spoke from experience. What had etched the worry lines on his forehead?

"Has anything like that happened to you?" she asked.

"Not to me, exactly. I don't have children and I'm not married. It happened to my aunt. My cousin ran away from home many years ago, and we never heard from her again."

"I'm sorry," she said.

"Ms. Vasquez?" Dr. Shaffer came down the hallway and stood in front of Adelina.

Adelina stood up. "Yes, Doctor?"

"Ms. Parker has pulled through. We've managed to stabilize her, and she's regained consciousness. You may go in and see her."

"Thank you, Doctor." Adelina turned to Dr. Luna. "It was nice talking to you again, Dr. Luna."

"Perhaps I will see you when I go down to the shelter."

Adelina glanced at Dr. Shaffer and felt her cheeks become red.

"We'll be waiting for your visit," she said to Dr. Luna, and then turned and headed down the hallway.

juana

Throughout the night Juana could hear the puppies whimper. When their crying got loud, Amá would wake up and go outside to check on them.

"Go back to bed," Juana told her. "Princesa is taking care of them."

"But what if they're cold, Juana? Why don't we bring them inside? They're so small and fragile."

"We'll do it tomorrow, Amá, now go to sleep."

Juana checked on the puppies before she went to work the next morning. The puppies cried and cried. They were crawling around, sniffing each other. Their mother was not there and they were trying to find her. Juana looked at the puppies one more time and then left for the train station.

When Juana came back from work, all the puppies were dead. She found her mother holding the empty can of jalapeños Juana had bought the day before.

"Amá, what happened to the puppies?"

Amá rocked herself back and forth. Her hair was matted, her face was streaked with dirt, and her dress was peppered with holes. The stench of alcohol seemed to have permanently soaked into her pores.

Now Abuelita Elena had every right to call her a beggar. Amá went from person to person trying to get money to buy beer or tequila.

"Princesa didn't come back," Amá said. "I went looking for her, but I didn't find her. Now what kind of parent abandons her children?"

"Maybe something happened to her," Juana said.

"Well, when I came home all the puppies were crying and crying. They cried so much, Juana. They were starving, the poor things, and there was no food in the house. Nothing, except this can." Amá raised the empty can and showed it to her. Juana sniffed the pungent smell of spicy vinegar.

"You should have seen how they sucked on the jalapeños. They were so hungry." Amá hugged her legs closer to her and rocked back and forth. "Poor little puppies. Poor little puppies. Poor little puppies. So hungry and unloved."

On her eighth day of work, Juana left home one hour earlier. She took with her a bucket and a long bamboo stick with a hook tied at the end. As she made her way down to the train station she cut down the fruit of the guamúchil trees growing alongside the river. By the time she got to the station she had a bucket full of guamúchiles. She needed to earn more money for her trip.

"What is that for?" Doña Josefina asked when Juana got there. She pointed a dough-covered finger at the bucket.

"I'm going to sell guamúchiles," Juana said. "I hope it's okay with you, Doña Josefina."

After a moment Doña Josefina asked, "What do you do with the money I pay you, Juana?"

Juana hoped Doña Josefina didn't think she felt underpaid.

"I buy food for me and my mother. She hasn't been feeling well lately, and I'm trying to help out."

"I see. Well, all right then, go ahead and sell your guamúchiles. You can put them there, by the table, so people can see them."

"Thank you, Doña Josefina."

"Juana, have you thought about putting your mother in Alcoholics Anonymous?"

Juana looked down at the ground. Everyone in town had started calling Amá La Borracha, the drunk. She was no longer Doña Lupe, or la señora García. Now she was La Borracha. The town drunk.

"My mother will be fine," Juana said, thinking about the coffee can she'd begun to fill with pesos for the trip. As soon as she could get Amá out of this town, she knew her mother would be fine.

"I'm sorry, Juana, I didn't mean to pry into your personal life, it's just that I worry about you. Your mother has gone through a lot. Since your father left—"

"My father has not abandoned us," Juana said, but this time her words lacked conviction. She was tired of defending her father.

• • •

After work, Juana came home to an empty shack. She thought about going to look for Amá, but there were clothes to be washed, dinner to be made, and trash to be swept up; she decided to wait a little longer and see if she came home on her own.

She gathered the dirty clothes and put them on top of her blanket. After she tied the corners to make a sack, she put the bundle on her head and made her way down to the river. She passed by the vacant lot where the kids were playing soccer and tried not to listen to their whispers and whistles. "There goes La Borracha's daughter," they said, and laughed.

Suddenly, the ball came flying her way and landed near her feet. One of the boys started running toward her to come and get the ball, but Juana lifted her foot and then kicked. The ball rose into the air in a perfect arc. It flew above the kids' heads and landed near the goalpost.

"Way to go!" one of the kids yelled. Juana continued walking toward the river and didn't look back.

The river was empty. Most of the women came in the morning to do their washing. Juana was glad she had the flat washing stones to herself.

The water was low, and the current didn't have the urgency it usually had when it rained, as if it were running away from someone. Juana didn't like to be inside the river when the water was high.

She got into the water and poured the contents of the sack onto the lavadero. She scrubbed her knuckles raw washing out the stains on her mother's dresses. Most of them were torn, and she made a mental note to mend them before she went to bed. Soon her legs hurt from standing so much, and her neck ached from having her head tilted down.

There were no more noises coming from the vacant lot, and she knew the soccer game was over and the kids had probably gone elsewhere to do some mischief.

She dunked the dresses into the water to rinse them one more time, wrung them, and put all the clothes back in the blanket.

When she got home Amá was still not there. Juana hung the clothes inside the house to dry, lit the candles, and started the fire. She cleaned the beans and put them inside a clay pot with water, which she then put on the brazier to boil. She splashed water on the floor so as not to unsettle the dirt as she swept. And still, her mother did not come.

Juana grabbed one of her mother's shawls and placed it over her head. She put out the candles and left the shack in search of her mother.

She walked from street to street, and didn't look at the kids playing hopscotch in front of their concrete houses, at the women who were outside embroidering servilletas while talking to their neighbors, or at the men who sat on the sidewalks playing dominoes or cards with their friends. She tried not to hear the sounds of a television drifting out to the street or the upbeat rhythm of a merengue being played inside the house she was now walking by.

She looked everywhere, yet there was no sign of her mother. She made her way to the other side of town, where the wealthier people lived. Where Don Elías and his wife lived.

The street was deserted. Juana stopped walking to catch her breath and sat down on a large rock under a jacaranda tree. She took off her sandals and massaged the soles of her feet. It was then that she saw a woman lying on the ground a few feet away from her. Flies danced around her. Her face was covered with long, dirty hair in desperate need of a good brushing, so tangled and matted. She wore a long dress full of holes, and some of the tears were held together with safety pins.

She didn't move.

Juana walked over to the woman and reached down to touch her hand. She screamed.

"Give me another beer," the woman said as she grabbed Juana's arm. "Give me another beer."

"Girl, get away from that woman," someone said from behind Juana. She turned to look at the couple standing behind her. The man looked at her and said, "That crazy woman comes here all the time. I'll get a police officer to come and take a look."

The man's wife nodded and told Juana to go home. Juana didn't speak, and the couple soon began to walk away, complaining about the drunk who came to their neighborhood every day. "She should be arrested," the man said.

Juana looked down at the woman on the ground, bent down and turned her over. She noticed the big wet stain in front of the woman's dress and tried not to breathe in the stench of vomit.

"Let's go home, Amá," she said. She wrapped her arms around her mother's waist and picked her up.

adelina

She met Diana on Christmas Eve the previous year. Adelina had hurried down the street. She was supposed to be at the shelter by now, but instead she'd gone to the Alley in downtown instead, hoping the stores would still be open so she could buy last-minute presents. Tonight the employees at the shelter were making dinner and handing out gifts. They had even rented *It's a Wonderful Life* to show to the women staying at the shelter.

Most of the stores were already closed, but a clothing store was open, and she bought a few blouses. Then she went into a hair accessories store and purchased nice combs, barrettes, and hairpins with shiny stones on them. She went into another store and bought socks and underwear.

As she finally made her way back to the parking lot, she glanced at her watch. It was already six. She was supposed to be helping with the cooking.

She decided to take a shortcut through an alley to the

parking lot on the next street. It was quiet and dark. She started to run, listening to the tapping of her heels echoing against the buildings on either side. She took small breaths. The whole place reeked of urine. Finally, she could see the end of the alley ahead.

One of her bags fell from her hands, and she had to go back to retrieve it.

"Hey, lady. Can you spare some change?"

Adelina turned around and saw a woman sitting on the ground, leaning against a wall. She picked up the bag and slowly walked toward the woman who was dressed in rags, and was holding an empty beer bottle. Adelina held her breath. The woman smelled of urine and alcohol.

"Spare some change?" the woman asked again.

"What's your name?" Adelina asked.

The woman didn't answer. She hugged her knees closer to her and shivered with cold.

"What's your name?"

"Diana," the woman whispered.

Adelina bent down in front of her. Diana made an attempt to move away, but Adelina grabbed her arm and held her there.

"It's okay, Diana. I'm not going to hurt you. Come with me. I'll take you to a place where you can have a nice Christmas dinner and something warm to drink."

Diana shook her head. "Just give me some change and go, lady. I don't need a Christmas dinner. I want to stay here, alone."

Adelina heard a noise coming from the other side of the alley. In the darkness, she could barely see three men walking toward her, laughing about something. She grabbed Diana's arm. She had to get out of there.

"Come with me, Diana. Just for tonight. Tomorrow, if you want, I'll bring you back here."

Diana looked at her empty beer bottle. "All right," she said. "Just for tonight."

Adelina helped Diana stand up and held on to her as they headed out of the alley.

juana

Juana remembered the times of long ago when the saints and La Virgen de Guadalupe had been there for them. But now, all the statues were covered with dust, and the flower petals had long ago shriveled.

"They never heard our prayers, Juana," Amá said. "Maybe our offerings of wildflowers and scented candles weren't enough." Amá walked up to the altar she had stopped tending long ago and picked up her black rosary. She cleaned the dust off with the corner of her dress.

"They haven't forgiven me my sin. That's why they punish me so, taking away my son from me. It's such a harsh punishment, Juana."

Amá picked up the statue of La Virgen de Guadalupe and looked at it. "I must try to offer something more powerful than prayers and tears. But what can I offer them, Juana, for them to forgive me and help me get my son back?"

Juana didn't reply. What could her mother do for her sin to be absolved?

"It'll be Semana Santa in a few weeks, right, Juana?" Amá said.

It was already mid-March. This year, Holy Week would take place in early April. "Yes, soon it'll be Semana Santa," Juana said.

Every year during Semana Santa, the townspeople reenacted the events that led up to Christ's crucifixion, his death, and his resurrection. The most important event was the procession held at the church in the center of the town. Juana had seen the procession only once. Apá never liked to watch it. He preferred instead to stay home and roast peanuts on the brazier. But three years ago Juana had asked to attend the celebrations. She'd been especially curious that year because she'd been attending her catechism classes and the priest had talked on and on about the passion of Christ.

"I wish you wouldn't see such things," Apá had said. "But I'll take you so that you can decide for yourself."

The procession was a reenactment of the day Jesus Christ carried the cross to his crucifixion. Some of the townspeople dressed up as Jesus, Virgin Mary, the Nazarenes, the guards, the apostles, and Pontius Pilate. But what stayed in Juana's mind was the image of the flagelantes, men and women self-flagellating with metal-pointed whips. These were the penitentes, people who showed their faith or penitence by inflicting pain on themselves. The image of their bloody backs lingered in Juana's memory. She wished she'd never seen the procession. For many months afterward, she had recurring nightmares about the flagelantes. She could see the whips swinging up and down in the air, digging into human flesh.

• • •

Amá stopped begging in the streets. She'd gone to Doña Martina and asked her for herbs that would purge her of the desire to drink, and she started taking baths again. At night, she stayed up surrounded by candles, making something she forbade Juana to see.

"It is my last plea," she'd told Juana. "My last plea for absolution."

And now, Juana rarely saw her. Sometimes Amá wouldn't come home until the next day, saying she'd been praying all night with Doña Martina.

The day of the procession Amá left the house early in the morning. "Be a good girl, Juana, and mind the house. I'll be back later tonight. I'm going to pray at the foot of the statue of Our Virgin Mary. I am sure that she, who also suffered the loss of a son, will help me get my child back."

Juana nodded and watched her mother leave. She went down to the river to wash their dirty clothes and spent the better part of the morning trying to catch an iguana she'd spied on a branch of a guamúchil tree. Amá loved fried iguanas smothered in chile guajillo sauce. Juana wasn't successful at catching it. She threw stones and managed to knock the iguana to the ground, but it crawled away and hid under the bushes.

Juana went back to the shack and busied herself with cleaning. She picked up the sandals her mother had left by the door and as she put them under her cot, she was surprised to find a little paper bag underneath there. It contained small metal nails. She wondered what her mother would need nails for.

Her attention was then drawn to the sound of hooves

outside. She looked out to see Doña Dolores. Her two sons rode on the donkey while Doña Dolores walked beside them. She was bringing drinking water from the well. The water splashed inside the metal containers hanging on each side of the donkey.

"Good afternoon, Juana," Doña Dolores said as she came to a stop in front of the shack.

"Good afternoon." Juana was glad Doña Dolores had come. The clay water pot was almost empty, and Juana hated going to the community well and carrying pails of water all the way back to the shack. Usually the buckets would end up only half full, most of the water spilling on the way home.

"This is my last stop," Doña Dolores said. "I must go home now and cook a quick meal for my children. I'm running a bit late today. And it's almost time for the procession."

Juana listened politely, but remained silent.

"Have you heard from your father?" Doña Dolores asked.

Juana shook her head.

"I'm sorry, Juana," Doña Dolores said. After an awkward silence she added. "You shouldn't pay attention to what people say, about your father having abandoned you. I knew Miguel well. He was a good man. And perhaps I shouldn't say this, but there are other possibilities to be considered."

"Like what?" asked Juana.

"Many people have died trying to get to the other side, Juana. Like those men who were in the news a few days ago. Did you hear about it?"

"No."

"Well, two men drowned trying to cross the river. The

fools didn't know how to swim. I don't understand why they decided to cross that way."

"My father knows how to swim."

"Yes, I know. But what I meant is that sometimes bad things like that happen and, well, maybe you and your mother should resign yourselves—"

"Thank you for bringing the water, Doña Dolores, but I must get back to my cleaning." Juana took out money from her coin bag and gave it to Doña Dolores.

"Yes, yes, I must go home, too. I must see my husband before the procession." Doña Dolores closed her eyes for a moment, and Juana could see the painful expression on her face. "I just don't understand how he can do it."

"Do what?" Juana asked, curious.

"Whip himself. He's been doing it for five years now."

"Why does he do it?"

"To ask for forgiveness, Juana."

Juana pushed and elbowed her way through the crowd congregated in the streets. Her heart was beating fast. She pressed a hand against her chest. She kept feeling little pricks inside, as if a tiny sewing machine was stabbing her heart. She carried the paper bag with nails she'd found under her mother's cot.

She got to the church and pushed her way to the front. In her mind she kept hearing the words her mother once said: *I must try to offer something more powerful than prayers and tears. But what can I offer them, Juana, for them to forgive me and help me get my son back?*

She pushed her way along the procession route, trying to

find the penitentes. Finally she got to the agachados, men and women walking in a bent position with their ankles tied together, dragging heavy chains. Then she saw the flagelantes. They wore long black dresses cinched at the waist with a belt. The men were exposed from the waist up. The women's backs were bare. They walked the procession route barefooted, their heads covered with black hoods. And all of them had their backs covered in blood.

"Your mother told you not to come, Juana," Doña Martina said.

"I know what she's doing."

Doña Martina shook her head, in disapproval.

"Which one is she?"

Doña Martina didn't answer. Juana grabbed her arm.

"Which one is she?"

Doña Martina turned to look at her. "Fifth row, right in the middle."

Juana looked at the red streaks of blood on her mother's bare back. She took a step forward, but Doña Martina stopped her.

"Let her finish, Juana. Perhaps her sin will be absolved. It might be her salvation, and yours."

adelina

Adelina was sitting at one of the restaurant tables at the fish market, waiting for Sebastian. The wind was blowing her hair around her while the sun kissed her back. He took her to San Pedro to eat shrimp. Adelina had never been there. She'd been to many places, even as far as Watsonville, because she thought that perhaps her father had gone north to work in the fields.

"Dig in," Sebastian said when he brought the tray full of shrimp tossed with potatoes, green bell peppers, onions, all marinated in sauce.

Adelina's mouth watered just looking at it. He grabbed a shrimp and peeled it before popping it in his mouth. She tore a piece of garlic bread and slowly nibbled on it.

"So you went to Cal State L.A.?" he asked.

Adelina nodded. That had been the closest university to Dracula's castle. She would have never dreamed of going anywhere far away from it, even though Don Ernesto had insisted.

"And where did you go?" she asked him.

"UCLA."

"You've lived in Los Angeles all your life?"

"I'm from San Bernardino. I moved here when I started going to UCLA, and this is where I stayed."

Adelina watched him munch on another shrimp. She tossed her piece of bread aside and finally picked up her fork. He smiled.

"And your parents still live in San Bernardino?" Adelina asked.

Sebastian nodded. "Most of my family lives there. My brother lives in San Diego, and my sister recently moved to Berkeley to go to school."

Adelina searched for a potato. The food was delicious. And there was something special about both of them eating from the same tray.

"Why did you decide to become a doctor?" Adelina asked.

"When I was eight years old, my grandfather suffered a heart attack. I remember my mother screaming for help. I stood there, not knowing what to do, not knowing how to help my grandfather. He died. I made a promise to myself that I would learn how to help others."

"I'm sorry."

"Can we talk about you now?" Sebastian asked.

"There's not much to say," Adelina said.

He nodded, then turned to look at the row of boats lined against the dock.

"Isn't that one beautiful?" he asked.

Adelina took a deep breath and inhaled the salty scent. She looked at the boat Sebastian was pointing to. A small boat just waiting to journey out to sea. The seawater shimmered on its white surface.

juana

The baby cried and she saw them: Don Elías, Doña Matilde, and her little brother inside a clothing store. Juana hid behind the door and peeked inside.

"I like this one," Doña Matilde said.

"Yes, yes, that one will look great on my boy," Don Elías said.

"And what will you baptize him as?" the saleslady asked.

"His name is José Alberto Díaz," Doña Matilde said. "I've named him after my father."

"Oh, what a lovely name," the saleslady said.

His name is Miguel García, Juana thought. *Miguel García. Miguelito García. My brother.*

Juana wondered if Amá knew about the upcoming baptism. She didn't talk about Miguelito much. All she did now was pray the whole day, just like she had done before, if not more. She had placed the whip still soiled with her blood at the foot of the statue of La Virgen de Guadalupe, so that She wouldn't forget Amá's plea.

The day of the baptism, Juana went to work as usual. She worked extra hard, trying to push aside the bitter thought that today would mark Don Elías's triumph over her mother. She wondered if the baby Doña Martina and Amá had gone to deliver had finally been born. Juana had asked Doña Martina to stay with her mother all day. Keep her busy. Keep her away from that church.

At three o'clock Doña Josefina told Juana she could go. Juana grabbed her usual share of quesadillas and walked home.

The shack was empty. She wondered what time Doña Martina and Amá would get home. She busied herself counting the pesos she was saving inside the coffee can, and wondered how much more money she needed for the trip. She and Amá had to leave soon.

There was a knock on the door. Juana opened it to find Doña Martina, alone. She was agitated, and she took deep breaths to calm herself. She had been running.

"Where's Amá?" Juana asked.

Doña Martina shook her head. "I don't know, Juana. We were at Julia's house, waiting for the baby to be born. And your mother just kept looking outside. Then she told me she was going to the outhouse and left. She never came back. I couldn't go look for her, Juana, the baby was due any minute. As soon as Julia delivered and I knew she was okay, I came here, hoping Lupe was with you."

Juana went to get a glass of water for Doña Martina.

Doña Martina took a drink. "Let's go look for her, Juana. I have a bad feeling about this."

Juana nodded. She knew where her mother had gone. But she didn't know what her mother had done.

Two police cars drove past them as they made their way to the church. The sirens left Juana's ears ringing. She held on to Doña Martina's arm, as if she were the old woman instead of Doña Martina.

There was a crowd gathered outside the church, some people crying, others shaking their heads, crossing themselves. Juana couldn't hear what they were saying. She saw Doña Matilde crying, with her one-year-old brother in her arms. Three police officers were standing by her, asking questions.

"She just showed up and tried to take my son from me," Doña Matilde told them.

"And do you know this woman?" one of the officers asked.

Doña Matilde shook her head, and between tears said, "She was drunk. She was talking nonsense. And she pulled a knife out of nowhere."

The church doors swung open and Amá came out, handcuffed, her dress covered in blood. Three judiciales walked alongside her, dragging her to the police car.

Juana ran, crying. "Amá? Amá? What did you do, Amá? What did you do?"

A judicial put his hand up to stop her. Juana kept running and grabbed her mother.

The officer slapped her hand away. "I said stay away!"

Juana looked down at the blood on her hands.

"They didn't hear my prayers, Juana," Amá said as the police officers dragged her along. "I begged him to give me back my son. He hit me and tried to throw me out."

The judiciales tried to push Amá into the car, but Amá fought them and kept talking to Juana. "What else could I do? He could do nothing worse to me than what he already did."

The judiciales pushed Amá into the car and slammed the door shut.

"Let my mother go! Let her go!"

The baby cried. Juana turned around and saw Doña Matilde standing behind her, looking at Amá.

"Take that murdering bitch away!" Doña Matilde screamed. "Let her rot in jail!"

Juana lay crying in her cot in a fetal position. Her heart hurt, as if restrained in a yoke. Her beautiful mother in jail. Her body shuddered.

Why had Amá killed him? Why?

She should have stayed with Amá yesterday. She should have stayed and not gone to work. Then Amá would never have done such a thing. Never. And right now they would be home together.

She walked to the altar and looked at the whip at the foot of the statue of La Virgen. She pulled her dress up and threw it on the floor. She got down on her knees, wearing only her underwear. A gust of wind blew in through the bamboo sticks and kissed her bare back. She shivered.

The saints wanted her blood, too. Maybe then they would finally listen to her prayers.

Juana took her mother's blood-soaked whip. She raised the whip high above her and brought it down hard on her back.

Two weeks later, once the wounds on her back had healed, Juana made her way down to the train station. She walked over the tracks, the gravel crunching under her feet. The morning sun shone bright, drying the last beads of dew clinging to the leaves of the wildflowers growing alongside the tracks.

How many times had she been inside the passenger cars, selling quesadillas and tacos? But when the whistle blew she always had to run back out. Many times she had watched the people climb inside and wave good-bye to their families from the windows. Everyone was always going places, always saying good-bye. And now, it was Juana's turn. For the first time in her life, she would get to ride the train.

The station was crowded with vendors and people. Juana showed her ticket to the attendant and went inside. She carried a sack filled with a few clothes and her coffee can full of pesos. She made her way down to the third-class section and sat.

Someone knocked on her window. It was Doña Martina and her granddaughter. Juana quickly stood up and lowered the glass down.

"I came to give you this," Doña Martina said. She stood on her toes and handed her a map. It was the map she'd once used to show Juana where El Otro Lado was. "So that you don't lose your way, Juana," she said.

"Thank you, señora."

"My granddaughter and her husband are going to move into your shack tomorrow. She will help me take care of it."

Juana nodded.

"Don't worry about your mother, Juana," Doña Martina said. "I'll take care of her. You just keep yourself safe, and your head clear. The road is dangerous." She handed Juana a small bundle she'd made from a handkerchief. Juana reached for it, wondering what it was. Something inside the bundle jingled. Coins. She handed it back to Doña Martina.

"I can't take your money, señora," Juana said.

Doña Martina shook her head. "You might need it, Juana. Don't worry about me. God will provide." She handed Juana a piece of paper. "Memorize this phone number. It's to Don Mateo's store. He'll deliver any messages you leave me."

The train whistle blew. Doña Martina made the sign of the cross in the air and blessed Juana. "Go with God, Juana." Doña Martina's voice was soft, like the cooing of doves.

Juana reached down to hold her hand and wondered if this would be the last time she would feel Doña Martina's calloused hand and smell the familiar scent of herbs that enveloped her.

On her way to Cuernavaca, Juana made an effort to remember her mother as she once had been, beautiful, full of life and faith.

She closed her eyes and tried to fall asleep, but sleep would not come. She wanted to drown in darkness, where no thought, yearning, or worries existed. She felt the taste of copper in her mouth. Fear tastes like that.

In Cuernavaca, she asked the taxi driver to take her to the bus station. She was surprised that this place looked so much like her hometown. The cobblestones, street vendors, the crazy drivers trying to outrun one another.

After an hour of waiting, the passengers boarded the bus.

Juana sat next to a lady who held her son on her lap. She noticed the beads of sweat glistening on the boy's forehead. He kept looking out the window, with longing and resignation. He was not much older than five, but his eyes looked old.

The woman tried to smile at Juana, but it seemed to take too much energy so instead she turned to look out the window, too, her eyes full of sadness, and fear. Juana wondered what she was afraid of.

Juana put her sack on her lap; her coffee can already felt a little bit lighter. She really hoped that the money would last her. The bus pulled out of the station and slowly made its way to the main road. Across the aisle sat a man busy reading a newspaper. In front of her sat a man and a small girl.

"Is El Otro Lado far away, Papi?" Juana heard the girl and paid attention.

"It's on the other side of the border, mi'ja," the father said. "When we get to Tijuana, a coyote will help us cross the border."

"What's the border, Papi?"

"Hills," her father whispered. "Hills and bushes, that's all it is. But we must walk across it."

"Papi, if it's just land, why can't we take the bus all the way there. Why must we walk across?"

"Because we don't have papers, Carmen. And even though it is just land, it represents a wall. We must go like thieves."

Juana wished she could ask what the father meant by that. Hills and bushes, that's what the border was. How strange.

The boy sitting on his mother's lap took deep breaths, as if he had been running fast and was now trying to calm himself.

"We're almost there, mi'jo, almost there," the mother said.

Juana looked at the woman, noticing for the first time the deep worry lines etched on the woman's forehead and around her eyes. The woman turned to look at her but said nothing. The boy got off his mother's lap and stood for a while. Then he got back on her lap again and took long breaths. He stood up again, although he didn't fit well between his mother and the seat in front of him.

He looked to Juana like a little lizard trapped inside a glass bottle. "We're almost there," the mother said again, with an urgency in her voice that surprised Juana. The man sitting across the aisle from her coughed and moved his newspaper aside so he could look at them. He looked at the boy for a moment, peering deep into the little boy's brown eyes. Juana noticed that the boy's pupils were dilated.

The mother picked up the boy and placed him back on her lap. She leaned against her seat and closed her eyes while holding on tight to her son. Juana closed her eyes, too, wishing the gentle rolling of the bus would lull her to sleep.

When she woke up from a dreamless sleep, the little boy was leaning against his mother, his eyes closed. Juana was glad he had finally fallen asleep. He'd been so restless. The mother looked out the window. Juana thought she was asleep, for she was so still, but her eyes were wide open. Did people sleep with their eyes opened? The bus jerked to the side. The little boy leaned against Juana, and she gently lifted him off. His head rolled forward. He hadn't even woken up.

"Arturito, mi'jo, we're almost there," the woman said again. But the boy kept his eyes shut tight, and didn't move. The

woman put her hand against his chest, and Juana felt her tremble beside her.

"Arturito, mi'jo, we're almost there," she said again, softly,
so softly, that Juana almost didn't hear her.

The man across from Juana put his newspaper down and
leaned closer to them. His breath smelled of mint, and she
wished she could ask him for a piece of candy to get rid of the
sour taste in her mouth.

"You must be strong, señora, for if you cry and make a
scene, you will cause a riot, and the bus driver would be forced
to stop and kick you out here in the middle of nowhere."

The woman turned to look at him. What was he talking
about? Juana wondered.

"You know how people are," he whispered. "They're afraid
of the dead."

The woman nodded, and she turned her head. Her hair
flapped against the wind coming in through the opened window. She put a piece of her shawl into her mouth and chewed it.
She chewed and chewed, and Juana wondered if she was hungry.

Why was the man talking about the dead?

The bus jerked again, and the boy leaned back against
Juana. She lifted her hand and touched his cheek.

"I think you should put the window up," she told the
woman. "Your son is cold."

"Nothing can hurt him now," the woman said. And she
stuffed a bigger piece of her shawl into her mouth.

Juana then noticed that his chest had stopped rising and
falling.

The woman's look pleaded with Juana to keep quiet.

• • •

When the bus pulled into Mexico City, Juana decided she would ask the father and daughter sitting in front of her if she could join them. They were heading to Tijuana, and they, too, were planning to cross to El Otro Lado.

Mexico City was full of speeding cars and cluttered with people rushing through the wide streets. Buildings competed for height and space. Trash lined the curbs and the sidewalks in colorful patterns. People slept underneath cardboard boxes on the sidewalk, not caring that they blocked the path, forcing pedestrians to walk around them.

Performers ran into the street whenever the traffic stopped. Some spit fire out of their mouths and others juggled balls or pins, their faces painted to look like clowns. Juana wondered if they did that to hide their real faces and not feel ashamed. Children walked around the street selling boxes of gum or newspapers. Others carried buckets and rags, and as soon as cars stopped they ran over to them and climbed on top to clean the windshields.

How hard it was to survive in this place, Juana thought.

The bus pulled into the station and when it came to a stop, Juana helped the woman throw a blanket on top of her dead son. She held on to the woman's arm until they climbed down the bus, never taking her eyes off the father and daughter, who were putting on their backpacks, getting ready to leave.

"Can you grab my bag?" the woman asked, pointing to the green satchel bag the bus attendant was taking out of the luggage compartment. Juana quickly grabbed it and threw it over her shoulder.

"I'll walk you in to the lobby," Juana said. The woman nodded and followed her. Juana wondered what the woman was going to do. When they got there she noticed that the father and daughter were purchasing their tickets to Tijuana. She wanted to run over to them and buy a ticket for the same bus so she could stay with them. Instead, she turned to look at the woman who was looking around the station as if she didn't know what she was doing there, with her dead son in her arms.

The father and daughter went into the back part of the station where people were boarding the buses.

"Is anyone going to pick you up?" Juana asked the woman. She shook her head.

"I have a cousin here who lends me her son's medical papers so I can take my Arturito to the doctor once a month. But she lives on the other side of the city, and she didn't know I was coming back so soon. I don't think those papers are of any use to me now."

"What are you going to do?" Juana kept looking at the boarding gate.

"I don't know. I-I have no money. My cousin usually lends me money to go back to Cuernavaca."

They both stood looking at the floor, not knowing what else to say. A groan tore from the woman's throat and she began to shake. The tears she could not shed in the bus suddenly spilled out of her eyes and streamed down her cheeks. "I need to take him home. I need to take him home. He's so cold, my little son, so, so cold."

She ran her fingers through the boy's hair and then rocked him in her arms, as if he were sleeping.

"Wait here," Juana said. For the last time she looked at the boarding gate and then turned around and walked over to the ticket window. "Give me a ticket to Cuernavaca, please."

"Gate six," the man said. "It leaves in half an hour."

Juana took out her coffee can and grabbed a bunch of pesos. She dropped them on the counter and started to count them. She looked at the man and noticed he was trying to hold back a smile.

"Here you go," she said.

"Sorry you had to break your piggy bank," the man said, and then threw his head back and laughed.

Juana ran back to the woman, who was leaning against the wall, struggling with the weight of her son as if he weighed three hundred pounds. Juana knew it was her sorrow that had taken her strength away.

"Come with me," Juana said. She helped the woman to the seats in the lobby.

"I need to go to the restroom," the woman said a few minutes later. Juana suddenly didn't know what to do. She knew the woman couldn't take the boy in with her. She gulped.

"Give him to me. I'll hold him for you." She extended her arms and the boy was laid on them. Juana held him close against her, trying to keep him warm. He looked so peaceful, and she noticed the corners of his mouth tilted into a smile.

Juana waved good-bye to the woman and watched the bus turn the corner. Her sack was lighter now, the coffee can almost empty. After she bought her ticket to Tijuana she threw it away. She exchanged the pile of coins left inside the can for bills, rolled them up, and stuffed them into her bra.

The ride to Tijuana would last three days. That's what the man at the ticket window had told Juana. The father and daughter had left without her, and now she had to travel alone, in a bus full of strangers. She wondered how the woman was bearing with her son. Juana knew she'd done the right thing, and yet she still wished she had all her money and that she was riding in the same bus as the father and daughter who were on their way to El Otro Lado.

The sun went down and soon everyone fell asleep, except Juana. As they traveled throughout the night the constant jerking of the bus kept chasing her sleep away.

Juana was the first one to get off the bus in Guadalajara. As she leaned against the wall to stretch her back, it felt as if a thousand little ants were crawling on her legs. She walked the numbness off by going in search of food. She hadn't eaten for nearly a day now. Her stomach had constantly growled in loud disapproval.

She followed the aroma of cecina broiling on the grill wafting into the station. She chose the food stand with the shortest line and waited her turn. She put one foot above the other, wishing the line would move faster. She took deep breaths and savored the spicy smell of chiles roasting.

Four more people to go and she would be next.

"Me da una caridad, por favor?" An old blind man put a tin cup close to her face and waited.

"I don't have change," she told him. But he only thrust the

cup closer, almost hitting her cheek with it. The wrinkled hand shaking in front of her reminded Juana of Doña Martina's hands. She followed the darkest vein bulging from the skin up his arm, until it disappeared beneath his old shirt. She found it again throbbing at the base of his neck. She looked at it for a moment, and then looked at his face, into his vacant eyes. They looked to the side of her, empty.

Juana thought about the few bills she had left and shook her head. "I'm sorry. I really don't have any coins to give you."

Three more people.

The old blind man made his way into the station with a walking stick to guide him. Farther down the street a woman with a child tied to her back with a shawl was putting out her hand to all the passersby.

"Una limosnita, por favor. Una limosnita, por favor."

Two more people.

How much time do I have left? Juana would rather go hungry than miss her bus. She turned around and was about to leave the line when finally the person in front of her left and it was now her turn.

"What would you like to order?"

"I want three tacos and a tamarind drink, please."

Ever so slowly the lady picked up the tortillas and filled them with meat. She stirred the water container for too long. She filled up Juana's cup one scoop at a time.

Hurry. Hurry.

"Here you go, niña."

Juana snatched the bag and cup and scurried back into the station. How much time did she have?

"Hey, watch it!"

The suitcases in front of her almost toppled over. Her drink spilled and the tamarind drink soaked into her dress.

"Dumb kid, watch where you're going."

The man pushed his suitcases forward. Juana ran again, and when a boy pushed his dolly in front of her she swerved to the left trying to avoid it.

"We have to catch that bus, girl."

Juana turned around and saw one of the passengers from her bus. Since he was tall and fat, he easily pushed people aside. She followed him, staying close enough to run through the space people made for him as they opened up like a zipper. A dolly with a mountain of suitcases was pushed in front of him, and he swerved to the right, bumping into the old beggar and knocking the tin cup from his hands. Coins fell on the linoleum floor like rain. They rolled away in every direction.

"Where's my cup? Where's my cup?" The old man reached out his hands and grabbed Juana's arm.

"I'm sorry," she said.

He got down to the floor and put his walking stick next to him. He ran his fingers over the floor, trying to find his coins. The fat man looked at Juana, and then looked at the boarding gate. She knew they didn't have much time left.

"Come on, girl. We'll miss the bus," he said.

"Move out of the way, old man." Someone almost tripped over the old beggar crouching low on the ground, frantically trying to find his coins. A whole day's worth of asking for money had rolled away from him. And now he would not eat.

Juana dropped to the floor and snatched the coins people were kicking as they hurriedly walked by.

She looked up, and the fat man was gone. She found the tin cup and dropped a few more coins into it. When she couldn't see any more coins she helped the old man get up and took off running.

Please be there. Please be there. Please be there.

"Hey, where's your ticket?"

Juana ran past the guard standing at the boarding gate and didn't turn back to see if he was coming after her. Line 9 was empty. Maybe it moved. She went to Line 10, Mexico City. Line 11, Tepic. Line 12, Hermosillo.

"Sir. Please, sir. Where's the bus to Tijuana?" Juana clutched the guard's arm, panting for air.

"Tijuana? Oh, it just left about a minute ago."

Juana let go of his arm and ran out of the parking area. Her bag of tacos fell from her hand, but she had no time to pick it up. She pushed people aside, not caring about the things they yelled at her. She could see the bus making its way down the street, slowly, being careful not to run over the pedestrians crowding the sides of the street.

The sidewalks were small and crowded, so Juana ran into the street and ignored the cars honking at her. She ran faster.

"You're going to get run over!" someone yelled.

Almost there. Almost there. The bus seemed closer now. When she got to the intersection the transit police guard standing in the middle of the street held up a white gloved hand at her side of the street and let the other cars pass by. A blur of white, blue, red, and yellow passed by her. And the bus became smaller and smaller as she stood there waiting for the gloved hand to go down.

She dove into the street. Cars swerved right and left trying to avoid hitting her.

"What are you doing?"

"Get off the street!"

The bus got smaller and smaller.

"Wait. Please. Wait!"

It finally pulled into the main highway. And at that point she stopped running. She leaned against a wall and clutched her ribs, which were throbbing with pain.

At night, the bus station was as quiet as a church. A few people sat scattered throughout the lobby, their heads hanging to the side in an uncomfortable sleep. Others were spread out on the floor on top of flattened cardboard boxes. They used newspapers as blankets and their arms for pillows.

Juana wondered where it would be best to sleep. If she slept on a chair she knew tomorrow she would have a severe neck pain. And if she slept on the ground, her back would hurt from lying on the hard, cold floor. She thought about her sack of clothes, and the sweater inside it. Who would take it now that it was riding the bus without her?

The people sleeping on the ground were men. And only one of the people sleeping on the chairs was a woman. She was an older woman covered with a black rebozo. Her long black braid curled around her neck, almost like a scarf. Juana made her way to her and sat a few chairs away.

The next bus to Tijuana would be arriving at six in the morning. Seven hours.

Juana glanced at the security guard standing at the entrance to the station, and she felt safe. She put her feet on top of the chair and hugged her legs, letting the skirt of her dress cover them as far down as it could go. She rested her head on her arms and closed her eyes.

The echo of footsteps vibrating against the walls, the screeching of tires, engines roaring to life, someone coughing uncontrollably, the serenade of snores, suitcases being dragged across the linoleum floor . . .

Those were the sounds Juana heard at the bus station throughout the night. She couldn't sleep. She was afraid to wake up and find that her bus had again left without her.

The security guard was walking around the station. She noticed that he was not the same one she'd seen a few hours ago. The other was an older man with a mustache and friendly eyes. This one was young, and he was now kicking the men sleeping on the floor and telling them to wake up.

"This isn't a hotel," he said. "Get up, get up."

Juana looked at the clock above the reception desk and saw that it was two in the morning. Four more hours.

"Please," a man told the guard. "It is late, and I'm tired."

"Sit on a chair or get out of the station," the guard said. The man gathered the sheets of newspaper he'd used as a blanket and went to sit across from Juana. When the security guard finished walking around the station, there was no one sleeping on the floor. Everyone was now sitting on the chairs, their heads bobbing, their tired bodies limp. Juana trembled with cold. She rubbed her hands and blew hot air into them. The man grabbed some of his newspaper sheets and gave them to her.

"Gracias," she said, as she wrapped herself with the newspaper. The man fell asleep. His snores were like a song, like one of the boleros Amá liked. She listened to them and tried to sing along, but the words wouldn't come.

adelina

Adelina sat beside Don Ernesto's bed and watched him sleep. They'd celebrated his eighty-third birthday two days ago. Frail now, Adelina had invited him to live with her but he had remained at Dracula's castle, insisting he must continue caring for his animals.

She visited him almost every day, especially now.

Don Ernesto stirred awake and smiled when he saw her. He held his hand up and touched her cheek. Adelina closed her eyes and put her hand over his. She put her head down on his chest and let Don Ernesto massage her scalp.

"What's the matter, child? You've been so thoughtful these last few weeks. Are you still reluctant to have a relationship with your young man?"

Adelina smiled. It always amazed her that Don Ernesto could read her so well. She sat up and looked at him.

"I've known you for fourteen years, Adelina. And in all that time I've never heard you talk about any young men. You've never gone out with anyone, never made friends—"

"I had no time for friends, Don Ernesto. Whatever time I had when not in school I spent looking for my father."

"Adelina, not even for love can you stop searching for your father?"

"Not even for love."

"Love is hard to find. You must not let it go. Don't waste your youth searching for a ghost."

"My father is not a ghost. I will find him."

"And when you do, then what? Will you be able to make up for all that wasted time? Will you be able to go back to your young man, hoping he's waited for you?"

Adelina was quiet for a moment. "I don't expect anyone to wait for me, Don Ernesto," she said. "There are things I have done. Things I cannot forget. There were men in my past, and my memories of them will never let me be free."

Don Ernesto reached for her hand. "Promise me you will give yourself a chance to be happy with this young man."

"But Don Ernesto—"

"Hush, mi'ja. I am an old man, and I will not be in this world much longer. The only thing I desire is to know you will not be alone. Humor this old man."

"Está bién, Don Ernesto. I promise. I promise I will try."

juana

The bus pulled off the highway and made its way into a small town. The headlights of the bus bounced up and down on the uneven dirt road. Around them, lights glimmered in the darkness, and it reminded Juana of the fireflies dancing around the bushes near the river at home.

"Where are we?" Juana asked the man sitting beside her. They'd been traveling for almost two days now, and she wondered when they would ever get to Tijuana.

"We're in the outskirts of Guaymas," the man said. "In the state of Sonora."

"Thank you," she said. Some people began stirring and talking in quiet voices. A few got up and took down their bags and suitcases from above.

Juana took out the map she'd bought during one of their stops. She was now only a few centimeters away from Tijuana. But how many kilometers away was she from her father?

• • •

The bus was pulled over by soldiers at the checkpoint farther up. Juana saw their flashlights waving, cutting through the darkness inside the bus as they climbed into it.

"Good morning, everyone, we are from the Department of Immigration. We are performing a routine inspection and ask for your cooperation. Please have your identification cards ready."

People murmured under their breath. Zippers were opened, papers were shuffled. Juana heard gasps of fear.

But who was afraid of these men shining their flashlights into their eyes?

She was.

What state are you from? Where do you live? Where are you going? The soldiers asked as they made their way down the aisle.

The man sitting beside her opened his bag and pulled out his credentials and birth certificate. He turned to look at her and asked, "Don't you have your documents?"

Juana shook her head. "I lost them on my way here. I have nothing that says who I am. Why are they doing this?" She looked behind her and saw a woman crying.

"They are looking for illegal immigrants from Central America. Salvadoreños, Guatemaltecos. Anyone who is not Mexican."

A soldier finally stood in front of them and pointed his flashlight at them. He asked to see their papers.

The man handed his to the soldier.

"What about the girl?" the soldier asked.

"Please, sir," the man said. "She's my daughter, but her papers were lost in a fire."

The soldier looked at Juana and asked her name and where she was from. She was careful to give the same information she'd seen on the man's papers. The soldier nodded and continued walking.

She let out her breath. The man patted her shoulder and smiled. "You speak like a real Mexican, girl, that's what saved you."

Juana turned to look at the soldier who was asking a woman questions, but she couldn't stop crying. The soldier pulled the crying woman to her feet and pushed her to the front of the bus. When she was almost at the door, she dropped to her knees and begged him to let her go.

"Por favor. I've come so far now. I've paid so much. Please. I'm almost there. Almost there. America!"

The soldier shook his head and pulled her to her feet again. He pushed her out the door.

When the bus pulled back into the highway, six people with tear-streaked faces were left behind, surrounded by soldiers.

The streets of downtown Tijuana were crowded with vendors and people. So many people elbowing each other on the sidewalks. When the bus finally pulled into the station Juana let everyone go before her, most of them looking as if they had somewhere to go, someone to be with. Others lingered behind, looking lost, like her.

When she pulled herself off the seat a sharp pain ran up her spine. Three days sitting on the bus. Her legs almost buckled over, as if they'd forgotten how to walk.

She wondered what she should do now. She had enough money for one meal. Tonight she would have to sleep at the station.

She made her way out to the street, wondering how one went about finding a coyote. Did they work in travel agencies? Could she just walk up to them and ask them if they remembered seeing her father?

And how would she describe her father to them? She thought hard about this, trying to remember what her father looked like.

But her memory of him was like smoke.

adelina

For a long time, Adelina refused to touch the inheritance—close to six thousand dollars—Don Ernesto had left her. She didn't want to accept that he was really gone. She'd wept for him for many nights.

Adelina eventually hired a retired police detective with Don Ernesto's money. At first, the detective had found false leads. But one November day he called to give her the news she'd wanted to hear.

"I think I've found him," Detective Brian Gonzalez said. "He's in Watsonville, working in the fields."

"Are you sure?" Adelina asked, remembering the trip she once took up north, stopping at Salinas, Castroville, and Watsonville. She had found nothing then. How could she have missed him?

"I've seen him," Detective Gonzalez said. "He has the same name as your father, and he came to the United States around the same time he did."

"Did you talk to him? Did you ask him about me, about my mother?"

"Uh, there's a problem, Adelina."

"What happened?"

"He doesn't remember anything. He was in a hit-and-run accident a long time ago, lost his memory, and he hasn't recovered it. He says he sees flashes in his head, images of a woman, a young girl."

"But he doesn't know who they are?"

"No. He said he's been waiting for someone to come look for him. He's sure he was part of a family, but he doesn't know where to look. He'd only been in Watsonville for two days when the accident happened. And the only thing his neighbors got to learn about him was his name."

"I'm taking the Greyhound bus tonight," she said.

"I'll pick you up at the station," Detective Gonzalez said.

Adelina gently put the phone receiver back on its cradle.

Is that why her father never came home, because he couldn't remember where he came from?

How many times had she ridden a Greyhound bus? Too many to count. Always on her days off she'd go somewhere to look for her father. San Diego, San Clemente, San Luis Obispo, Santa Barbara. So many names of saints. But none of them had helped her find her father.

Adelina popped two sleeping pills and reclined her seat. While she waited for sleep to come, she tried to remember what her father looked like. She vaguely remembered his eyes, the shape of teardrops, always drooping. Even when he smiled he still looked sad.

Adelina looked out the window at the darkness outside. She could barely see the silhouette of mountains in the distance.

• • •

Detective Gonzalez was waiting for her at the small bus station in Watsonville. He asked if she wanted to rest and have lunch. Adelina knew it had been a long ride, and her body was sore. But she shook her head anyway.

"I want to see him."

Detective Gonzalez nodded and led her to his car. He drove her down a winding road off the highway. In the distance, Adelina could see strawberry plants growing in parallel lines. They got to a cluster of trailer homes surrounded by trees. Children played outside. A woman was hanging her wash on a wire that ran from her trailer to a tree.

The woman stared at Adelina and Detective Gonzalez. Adelina sensed her fear of strangers. She knew people who worked here in the fields were always afraid of being surprised by la migra.

"Good morning, señora," Detective Gonzalez said. The woman nodded and turned back to her laundry.

"She's very tightlipped," Detective Gonzalez said. "Wouldn't answer any of my questions."

They knocked on a door and waited. Adelina tried to steady herself by taking deep breaths. Her father was probably on the other side of the door.

An older woman opened the door. She wore an apron over her dress, and Adelina sniffed the smell of beans boiling in a pot.

"Detective Gonzalez," the woman said as she dried her hands with a kitchen towel.

"Good morning, Señora Gloria. May I introduce Ms. Adelina Vasquez?"

Adelina reached out and shook the woman's hand.

The woman looked puzzled but nodded and led them into the small living room. She motioned for them to sit on the couch. Adelina did so, sinking into the worn-out cushions. She gripped the armrest with her hand and pulled herself back out.

"He went to get his hair cut," Gloria said. "He'll be coming any time soon. He just wanted to look his best when you came."

Adelina looked at her, listening to the way she spoke about the man she hoped was her father. With too much familiarity. Intimacy.

"Do you live together?" she asked Gloria.

"I live here, yes," Gloria answered as she nervously twisted the kitchen towel in her hands.

"What I meant to say is are you his partner?" Adelina said, not wanting to use the words "my father" and "wife."

"Yes, señorita. I'm his partner."

Adelina turned to look at Detective Gonzalez. Why hadn't he mentioned this to her?

"Listen, señorita," Gloria said. "He can't remember anything about his past. We didn't know if he was married and had children. For many years we stayed as friends, thinking that someday soon someone would come to find him. But no one did. We are old, alone. A few years ago we decided to give ourselves a chance to be happy."

Adelina watched Gloria twist the towel in her hand, as if she were wringing the neck of a chicken.

"I've been so afraid this moment would come," Gloria said, before excusing herself and running to hide in the kitchen.

Adelina didn't know what to think. She'd seen Gloria's face, agony written all over it. It must be hard having a relationship with someone, knowing that someday the past would come to haunt you.

She heard whistling outside and immediately sat up, her eyes glued on the door. The knob turned slowly. Adelina pressed her hands together, as if in prayer. *Please let him be my father. Please.*

The door opened and in came the man she'd been waiting for. He leaned against the door and stared at Adelina.

She got to her feet, not knowing what to say to him. Her lower jaw trembled slightly before her teeth clenched inside her mouth.

"Buenos días," he said as he extended his hand to her. "I'm Miguel García."

"Good morning," Adelina said and shook his hand.

His hand was rough, like pumice stones.

juana

It was dark. In the distance, a mariachi was playing "La Malagueña." Juana sang the lyrics under her breath, being careful not to be heard. She hugged her knees closer to her, trying to keep warm.

She wished she was with her mother, eating beans and cecina with salsa, or that she was lying next to her on the cot, feeling the warmth of her mother's body seep into her own.

Instead, she was sitting on a park bench, cold and hungry, so far away from home. She had tried to stay at the bus station, but the station was closed down at night and she had been kicked out. She'd wandered around the streets, not knowing where to go. She had no more money left, and had yet to begin searching for her father.

The wind rustled the leaves of the trees around her. She rested her face on her knees and let her hair drop down over her like a shawl.

She looked up, startled by the sound of running footsteps.

She barely caught a glimpse of the girl that ran past her, darting into the trees. Then voices drifted toward her. Loud, angry voices. Male voices.

"I know she came this way!"

"Catch that bitch before she gets away with my wallet!"

Juana scrambled to her feet. She looked to the right and saw shadows moving. Their footsteps sounded much closer. The beam of a flashlight tore through the darkness and fell on her face.

"There she is!"

Juana turned around and took off running. She heard them coming after her and ran out of the park, stopping at the intersection. She had to cross the street and get away from them. She plunged into the traffic and zigzagged through it. Cars swerved trying to avoid hitting her.

"Get out of the street!"

Juana stopped to catch her breath and turned around. Two male police officers and another man were coming after her. Why were they chasing her?

"Stop, thief! Stop!" the man yelled.

One of the police officers blew his whistle as they ran across the street. Without another thought Juana started running, bumping into the people walking on the sidewalk. She turned into an alley and kept running. She heard them behind her. They were so close now.

Heavy arms surrounded her, and she was thrown to the ground.

"We've got you now, girl. We've got you."

Her arms were pulled behind her and handcuffs were put on her wrists.

"You've made a mistake!" Juana yelled. "You've made a mistake!"

Juana huddled against the corner of the jail cell. She felt tears trying to seep through her eyes, but she wouldn't let them come out. She'd told them again and again. They'd made a mistake. She'd done nothing wrong, except trying to sleep on a park bench. And was there a crime in that? But the man kept insisting, kept asking her for his wallet.

The judiciales searched her, touched her most intimate places. She said again and again, "I didn't steal anything." The man had insisted she'd taken his wallet. They'd said she must have hidden it somewhere.

After the interrogation they threw her into a cell with three other female prisoners. Two of them seemed to be in their thirties, the other was young. Not much older than Juana. All of the women's faces were heavily painted. Their bright red lipstick had smeared. Their mascara stained their cheeks.

The girl wore a short black skirt made out of a shiny material and a red top with spaghetti straps. The other two women wore tight, short dresses. These were mujeres de la calle, prostitutes. Juana had seen some of those women before.

The youngest girl noticed Juana staring at them and made her way to the corner where she sat. When she bent down right in front of her, Juana could see the deep, purple bruises on the upper part of her arms, as if someone had gripped her hard and shaken her.

"What's your name?" the girl asked.

"My name's Juana García." The girl's eyes were a deep green, reminding Juana of the river back at home, the green fields, the green grass rippling in the breeze.

"And what's your name?" Juana asked.

"Adelina. Adelina Vasquez."

adelina

Miguel García kept his eyes on Adelina, and she kept her eyes
on him. She looked at every part of his face: his long pointed
nose, his almond-shaped eyes, his mouth that curved like a
bow, the deep grooves etched on the corners of his mouth and
on his forehead, his short gray hair.

"Please, sit down," he said. Adelina nodded and sank back
into the old couch. She felt herself sink more and more, as if the
couch had turned into a black hole that was sucking her in.

"I've prayed for this moment for a long time," Miguel said
as he sat down on a chair. "For all these years I've felt as if I've
been living in darkness."

"It must be so hard for you," Adelina said. "Not knowing
who you are, where you came from, or the people you loved
and who loved you."

"That has been the hardest part. To not know who I left
behind. Who was depending on me."

"Detective Gonzalez said you see things in your head.
Fragments of memories, perhaps?" Adelina said.

Miguel nodded. "It happens mostly when I'm asleep. I see a woman brushing her long black hair while she talks to me, but I can't hear what she says. I see a little girl who sits on my lap, asking me to tell her a story. I see hills, green fields. Sometimes I'm bathing in a river. Sometimes I see an old woman. But they feel as if they are just dreams."

Adelina remained silent, thinking about how hard it must be to always wonder if what you saw inside your mind were just figments of your imagination or if they were real.

"Are you my daughter?" he asked, suddenly. Adelina looked at his hands. He was clutching the armrest of his chair so tightly, his knuckles were white. Gloria came to stand beside him, and she, too, looked at Adelina as intently as Miguel.

Adelina knew what Miguel García wanted of her. He wanted his identity back. He wanted all those forgotten years back. He wanted to remember, to be able to look in the mirror and know where his roots were.

And she knew what she wanted of him. She wanted her freedom.

"I'm sorry," Adelina said. The words choked inside her, and her eyes filled with tears. Bitter tears full of disappointment. "You are not my father."

The moan didn't come from her mouth, but she felt as if it had. Miguel García covered his face with his hands. She saw his body tremble, saw his hopes shatter, saw Gloria wrap her arms around him, as if trying to hold the pieces together.

Adelina closed her eyes, let herself sink into the old couch, and listened to him weep.

juana

"So they threw you in here because they thought you stole something?" Adelina asked Juana.

Juana nodded.

"Carajo. Those sons of bitches always do things like that. They throw anyone in jail whether they're guilty or not."

"Why are you in here?" Juana asked.

"I, um, you know, I was working."

Juana looked down at the floor, embarrassed.

"You're not from here, are you?" Adelina asked.

"No. I just got here this morning."

"I got here three years ago," Adelina said. "What are you doing here in Tijuana?"

Juana looked down at her hands as she thought about her father. She felt as if something was stuck in her throat. Tears were threatening to spill from her eyes.

"I'm here to find my father. He left home two years ago. He came here to cross to El Otro Lado. But we never heard from him again."

Adelina reached out and stroked Juana's hair. Juana instinctively pulled back. It shocked her to feel someone's hand touching her with such tenderness. She remembered Amá used to touch her like that when things were good between them, before Anita died.

"You'll find him, you'll see," Adelina said.

Juana nodded.

Juana stayed in jail a day longer than Adelina. But once the charges against her were dropped and her named was cleared, she was told that she could go. Adelina was waiting for her at the entrance of the police station, just as she had promised.

"You're going to stay with me," Adelina said. "Doña Lucinda says she doesn't mind, as long as she gets her rent."

"Who's Doña Lucinda?" Juana asked.

"She's the owner of the place where I live."

"I don't have any money, Adelina, but I promise I'll get a job soon and help you."

"I know you will."

They walked across the street and waited at the bus stop. Juana watched the cars speeding by. She felt so small in this place, surrounded by all those tall buildings, and crowded by so many people.

"Adelina, why are you helping me?"

Adelina looked at the bus heading their way. "Because you're doing something I don't have the courage to do."

"And what's that?"

"To go look for my parents." Adelina took out the money she needed for the fare. The bus came to a stop in front of them.

"What do you mean?" Juana asked as they boarded the bus.

They made their way down the aisle and sat in the back of the bus, where it was less crowded.

"I ran away from home three years ago, when I was fifteen. I'm from El Otro Lado, as you call it. There have been many times when I've wished I could go back home. But how could I go back now? Look what I've become." Adelina looked away, but before she did Juana was able to see her eyes become glossy with tears. She looked at the fresh bruise Adelina had tried to conceal by putting extra makeup on her face. Where were all the bruises coming from?

"And why did you run away?" Juana asked, wondering if she should pry into Adelina's life. When she looked into Adelina's dark green eyes, though, she didn't feel as if she was looking into the eyes of a stranger.

"I fell in love," Adelina said. "But he was much older than me, and my father threatened to send me to live with my grandparents if I didn't leave him. So we ran away, here, to Tijuana."

"And where is he?"

"He comes to visit me once in a while, to collect his cut."

Adelina lived in an old apartment building not too far from downtown. The blue paint was peeling like dry husks, and the grass grew wild. Adelina said there were twelve rooms in the building, and mostly girls lived there. Girls like her. The girl who had shared the room with Adelina had gotten married to a client and left.

"Wasn't she lucky, Juana?" Adelina asked her as they walked down the hallway.

Noises were coming from behind the closed doors they

175

walked by. Grunting noises, beds squeaking. Juana heard someone laughing. Another crying.

A woman stood outside a door, smoking. As they approached
her, Juana recognized her as one of the women who had been
locked up in the cell with her.

"Hey, Veronica," Adelina said. "Remember Juana?"

Veronica nodded, blowing out the cigarette smoke and
watching it curl in front of her. "So, you decided to join us?"
she asked.

Juana didn't know what she meant. But she didn't like the
sound of the question.

"A virgin, huh? Oh, come on, don't be scared," Veronica
said. "You're young and have looks, although you're too much
on the skinny side. But I guess that'll be to your advantage.
You look so small and fragile," she said as she caressed Juana's
cheek. "Most men will find that fascinating."

"Come on, Veronica, you're scaring her." Adelina grabbed
Juana's hand and took her upstairs to her room. The smell of
cigarette smoke trailed behind them. Adelina headed to her
dresser and lit an incense stick. Juana breathed in the smell of
jasmine wafting into the air. It smelled like Amá.

Adelina pointed at the twin-size bed at the opposite end of
the room. "That one is yours," she said.

Juana nodded. She sat on the bed that was now hers and
bounced up and down. The mattress was old and the bed
squeaked when she sat on it, but it was better than the cot
she'd left behind.

Adelina walked up to her closet and took out a bright red
minidress.

"Are you going out?" Juana asked.

Adelina nodded. "Yeah, gotta work," she said in English. She turned to look at Juana and laughed. "Necesito ir a chambear. You know what? I'm going to teach you to speak English."

Juana had never heard English before. The words were so foreign. But she wanted to learn. Maybe her father had already learned to speak English. And wouldn't he be surprised, when she at last found him, to hear that his daughter could speak that foreign tongue also?

"Do you like what you do?" Juana asked.

"Nah, but I don't know how to do anything else. It's not that bad, once you get used to it."

Juana tried to look away when Adelina took off her clothes. She had never seen a naked woman before, not even her mother. But Juana couldn't help turning back and looking at Adelina's slender body. She wondered if in a few years she, too, would look like that.

"How long have you been doing this?"

"Almost three years. My boyfriend got me into this. We were so broke, and he couldn't find work. So one day he just brought his friends over and one thing led to another, and there they were, stuffing money into my boyfriend's hands, paying for me."

When Adelina turned, Juana saw a lot of scratches running down her back.

"Well, gotta run now," Adelina said as she finished applying a fresh layer of makeup.

"I want to go out. I need to start looking for my father."

"It's kind of late, Juana. You should start tomorrow."

"No, I think the sooner I start, the better." Juana got on her feet. "Can you tell me where I can find coyotes?"

Adelina whistled. "Yeah, some of them are my clients. But I must warn you, Juana. They are pretty tightlipped. The only way you can get them to talk is in bed. But anyway, come with me, and I'll point them out to you."

Adelina handed Juana a sweater but didn't take one for herself.

"Won't you be cold?"

"I need to show what I'm selling, Juana. I don't mind the cold. What I do mind is being hungry and penniless."

When they got to a bar, Juana couldn't help wrapping the sweater tighter around her. She felt eyes watching her. Too many eyes boring into her, as if trying to undress her. Men whistled as they made their way to the bar. Adelina sat on a stool and crossed her bare legs, letting the red fabric ride higher up her thighs.

She motioned for Juana to sit next to her. Men were soon upon them, offering to get them drinks.

"Hey, Adelina, you brought us a little lamb?" one of the men said.

Adelina shook her head. "Sorry boys, she's not in this business. She has another business that brought her here, actually."

"And what's that?" another man asked as he handed Adelina and Juana a beer. Adelina reached for hers, but Juana shook her head no.

"I'm looking for my father," Juana said softly, wondering if the men had heard her above the music.

"You're looking for whom?" one of them asked.

"My father. He came here two years ago to cross the border, but we haven't heard from him since."

The men shook their heads. "Sorry, girl, but I'm afraid I can't help you with that." Some of them turned their backs on Juana, others walked away. Adelina looked at her and shrugged her shoulders.

"It's going to be hard to get them to talk, Juana," she said.

Juana thought about Amá, about the things she had done with Don Elías, the things people used to say about her, the sin that weighed so heavily on her mother's back. Her mother had done what needed to be done.

Juana would have to do the same.

adelina

Adelina watched the flag swaying from a pole at the top of a hill. She wondered when it had been put up. It had not been there when she left the town seventeen years ago.

The bus slowly made its way down the mountains, heading down to the valley, where the town lay. Adelina became dizzy as the bus rode over the curves.

She kept her eyes on the town sprawled out below her, wondering how much it had changed. Would she know where to go? Or would she feel as if she had never been in this place before? Would she get lost?

The curves soon ended and the driver slowed down as they entered the town. People began to stir. Some got up and began to take their things out of the compartments above their heads. Adelina stayed in her seat, not moving.

Only her eyes moved, taking in the sight of the church towers rising above the buildings, the paved streets, the dirt roads, the marketplace full of vendors. She saw the taxicab drivers competing with one another for customers, saw a man selling churros at the corner, a woman selling fruit across the street, a young boy shining shoes, an old woman holding out her hand for alms.

Perhaps the town had not changed as much as she'd thought it had.

With the exception of a few new buildings, a few streets that were now paved, a few more houses occupying areas that had once been vacant, Adelina felt as if she had left just yesterday. Except now she was thirty-one, not fourteen.

"Well, we're finally here," the man sitting next to her said as the bus pulled into the station.

Adelina nodded.

"Hope you have a good stay," the man said as he stood up and joined the people who were getting off the bus. Adelina willed herself to stand up, too, and made her way out.

One by one people took their boxes, bags, or suitcases out from the luggage compartment. There was no attendant there to help them. Adelina looked for her green suitcase and caught a glimpse of it; it was squashed under a bulging duffel bag. She looked around her, wondering whose it was. She tried to move it aside, but she had the wooden box in one hand and she knew she would have to use both hands to push the bag off her suitcase.

"Permítame," someone behind her said.

Adelina turned and saw the young man with the droopy eyes standing behind her. She looked at his eyes that seemed sad even though he was smiling. She felt her stomach tighten.

"Thank you," she said as she moved to the side and let him fish the duffel bag out. He grabbed her suitcase and handed it to her.

"You're welcome," he said. He grabbed the bag and started walking away with it.

"I didn't realize it was your bag," Adelina said as she caught up to him. "It looks heavy."

"Actually, it's not that heavy. It's full of stuffed animals, that's why it's bulging like that."

Adelina laughed a nervous laugh. Why was she feeling like that?

"Why would you have a duffel bag full of stuffed animals?" she asked.

"My mother loves them. Every time I come to visit her I try to bring her as many as I can. That way they can keep her company while I'm gone."

They headed out to the waiting area. She saw him looking around, as if trying to find someone.

She looked only at him. Nobody was waiting for her. And even if someone had been, she still wouldn't have been able to take her eyes off this young man.

"Do you live here?" the young man asked as he stopped to put his bag down.

Adelina shook her head. "I'm visiting my mother, like you."

"Where do you live?" he asked.

"In Los Angeles, and you?"

Adelina watched his eyes roaming around the busy waiting area. So many people coming and going. He looked so eager to find the person who was waiting for him.

"I live in Mexico City. I'm studying at UNAM, and as soon as school lets out I come back here to be with my mom."

"And why doesn't she go live with you?"

"She hates living in a large city. Besides, I'll only be in the city until I finish school, then I'll come back here to be with her. Look, here she comes now."

Adelina turned around and looked in the direction he was pointing at. She felt as if the floor was giving way under her feet. He grabbed her shoulders to steady her.

"Are you all right?" he asked.

Adelina nodded and quickly moved away from him.

"Mamá!" he said, and then ran to hug the old woman who was slowly walking toward them, leaning on a cane.

Adelina looked at the woman's face. It was mapped with wrinkles. The hair was a light gray, almost white. Her body was bent, aiming at the ground beneath.

But there was no mistaking who the woman was. Now Adelina knew why the young man looked so familiar.

juana

"Are you sure you want to do this?" Adelina asked Juana.

She nodded. Adelina began to apply blue eye shadow on Juana's eyelids.

Juana looked in the mirror, watching herself change into a stranger. She was wearing a shiny black dress that fit so tightly on her body Juana couldn't tell where her skin ended and the dress began. She turned away from her image in the mirror and instead looked into Adelina's green eyes. She thought about the river back home. The deep green water. She remembered when she used to wash her clothes there with Amá. Or when she used to go fishing with Apá.

She thought about the stalks of corn swaying in the distance, and she could almost hear Apá telling her how much corn he'd harvested that day while they stood on the hill, looking down at the fields.

Yes, she was doing the right thing.

Adelina smiled at her. "There. You look beautiful."

Juana turned around and didn't recognize the young woman looking back at her.

"Juana, you really don't have to do this," Adelina said as she put her arm around her.

"It's been four weeks now, and I'm no closer to finding my father than I was when I first got here. There's no other way. Those men will talk. I will make them tell me what they know."

Juana swallowed her saliva in a big gulp. She felt the tears rush to her eyes and before she could stop them they began to run down her cheeks.

"Hey, hey, it's okay," Adelina said. "It's going to be okay."

Juana cried harder.

"Now, stop crying, Juana, you're going to ruin your makeup."

They looked at each other in the mirror. Juana smiled, before breaking into tears again.

The small hotel room her first client rented smelled like cigarette smoke, sweat, putrid water, and dirty feet. There was a full-size bed in one corner, covered with a spread stained with dark spots. The linoleum floor was pocked with holes, and was in one corner swelled up as if it were pregnant. Roaches scurried across the walls.

It will only be a while, Juana told herself. As soon as the door was closed, the man put his arm around Juana. Adelina had said he was one of the most popular coyotes in this area. He was the best one to start with, she'd said. Juana let herself be pulled into his embrace. Her mouth clamped shut when she felt his lips upon hers. But he probed with his tongue, and she had no

choice but to force her lips to open and let him in. He tasted of
beer, and Juana felt her stomach heave. She kept her eyes open
and let herself be kissed.

He was so much older than she. He was probably as old as
her father. Juana looked down at the floor while he kissed her
slender neck. She saw a roach pass by her foot, and she
instantly lifted it up and brought it down on the roach.

She didn't want anyone to see her shame. Not even
roaches.

"What did he tell you?" Adelina asked when Juana joined her back
outside in the street. Juana was trying hard to swallow her tears.

"He says that there are so many men who look like how I
described my father, he couldn't begin to tell me whether he
helped him cross the border or not." Juana crossed her arms
around her chest and shivered. The night was so cold, and she
wished she had a sweater.

"But there has to be something different about your father,
Juana. A scar, a mole, anything. Or even something he was
wearing, like a chain. I don't know. Didn't he bring anything
with him?"

Juana thought about the rainy morning when her father
left. She remembered how she had chased after him. She
remembered she had given him something.

"He brought a white rosary made with heart-shaped
beads," Juana said.

"Well, there you go, Juana. That's how you'll find your
father."

adelina

She was now only a few minutes away from her last stop. As the taxicab made its way across the bridge to the other side of the river, Adelina started feeling something flutter inside her stomach. Was it fear? She was afraid of seeing her mother. She knew she wouldn't like what she would see. It wouldn't really be her mother. It would be her mother's ghost. Her real mother had died many years ago. Only a shell remained, like a chest full of memories and longing.

She knew it was too late to save her mother. She would die soon, and in a way it would be best. She would no longer suffer. And once Adelina gave her her father's ashes, and once she told her the truth behind her father's disappearance, she knew that her mother would die in peace.

This would be Adelina's gift to her mother.

Peace.

And truth.

Her father had not abandoned them.

juana

The knock on the door startled Juana awake. She'd been dreaming about her mother. In her dream, her mother swung a whip high in the air, then brought it down on Juana's back. As she walked to the door, Juana could still feel her back contract with pain as the whip landed on it. She glanced at Adelina, who was still asleep in her bed. Before Juana could ask who it was, the door swung open. She didn't even attempt to greet the man who stood in front of her. It was Adelina's boyfriend, Gerardo.

"She's sleeping," Juana said. "Maybe you should come back later."

"It's eleven o'clock, it's time for you girls to get your lazy nalgas up," Gerardo said.

"Well, you're not the one who goes to sleep at four in the morning. Or later."

Gerardo waved Juana's words away. He leaned closer to her, grabbing her arm. "Calm down, chiquita. There's no need for harsh words. You and I could get along just fine if you weren't so defensive. I wanna be your friend." Gerardo said the last part in English.

Juana tried to recall the English words she'd learned and said, "I no need you for friend," before yanking her arm away. Gerardo laughed at her response.

It was impossible to hide how much she disliked Gerardo. At first she'd been civil with him, but she couldn't forgive him for treating Adelina so badly. And worst of all, for hitting her. She turned to look at him. He was looking her up and down, his eyes narrowing to slits. Juana felt an urge to slap that look off his face. He reminded her so much of Don Elías. Gerardo smiled at her, then turned and headed to Adelina's bed.

"Oye, tú, wake up, mujer. Stop being so lazy." He shook Adelina awake.

"Let her sleep," Juana said as she took a step toward him.

Adelina opened her eyes and rubbed them.

"It's all right, Juana, I'll get up," Adelina said as she yawned.

Juana shook her head. "I'm going downtown," she said as she headed to the door.

"Take your time," Gerardo said.

Every time Gerardo came over, Juana would go walk around downtown Tijuana, looking at all those golden-haired gringas people talked so much about in her town. How many times had they accused Apá of falling in love with a gringa and forgetting all about Juana and Amá?

As she made her way down Calle Revolución, Juana

looked at them and the people who walked with them. But no one ever looked like her father. The gringas' companions were other men like them, light-skinned and blue-eyed. Apá hadn't left them for a gringa. He couldn't have.

She walked from street to street, always looking at people's faces. Sometimes she would find men who, from behind, looked like her father. She would walk quickly, trying to catch up. But once she saw their faces, she would stop walking and watch them walk away, until they got lost in the crowd.

When she came back she found Adelina crying in bed. Sometimes she had a black eye, other times a swollen cheek, bruises on her arms or legs, a cut or a scratch on some part of her body. This time, she was rocking herself back and forth, holding a bloody hankerchief over her lip.

"Why do you let him do this to you?" Juana asked her.

Adelina curled into a fetal position and bit her thumb as she cried.

"One day he'll change," Adelina said. "He'll be like he used to be when we first met. I know he loves me. And I know one day he'll change."

Juana wondered what she could do to help Adelina come to terms with what she'd done so that she could go home. She sat on the bed and stroked Adelina's hair. She wished she could tell Adelina about all the times Gerardo had bothered her, tried to force himself on her. But she didn't want to hurt her more.

Instead, Juana said, "Adelina, you have a mother and father who love you, and an older brother who misses you. You should go home and forget all of this." She reached down and lifted Adelina's tear-streaked face. "You don't belong here."

Adelina shook her head in agreement. "I miss my brother the most. He looked after me a lot when he was still at home. But when he left for college I felt so alone without him. And that's when I met Gerardo."

Juana thought about her little brother. She wondered if she would ever get the chance to see him again, to call him "hermano."

"Then you should go back, for your brother."

Adelina shook her head. "I can't face them, Juana. Not anymore. You don't know how many times I've wished I could go back. But there are things that can't be undone, Juana. I made a choice, and I must live with it."

Juana lay down next to Adelina. Adelina put her head on Juana's chest and closed her eyes.

"I'm so tired, Juana."

"Go to sleep, I'll stay here and hold you."

As she held Adelina, Juana thought about what she'd said. *Some things can't be undone.* How true her words were. She couldn't turn back time to the day when she let Anita fall from her arms while she was sleeping. And just like Adelina, she, too, must live with it. How could she help Adelina forgive herself and go back, when Juana herself couldn't do the same?

Juana searched for weeks, looking for the man who had a blue film over his left eye. That was the only thing she remembered about him. When he'd picked her up that night at her corner,

Juana had stared at that eye, uncertain whether she should go with him.

What was it about that blind eye that bothered her so?

But the man was a coyote. He might know something about her father. Juana took his hand and let herself be guided to the nearest motel. She let him put her hand on his private area. She felt the calluses on his fingers scrape the tender flesh of her back. And when he began to undress her, Juana couldn't wait any longer and began to talk about her father.

"I'm looking for my father," she told him. The coyote didn't seem to hear her. He slid her underwear off her and began to caress the inside of her thigh.

"He came here three years ago to cross the border, but we never heard from him again . . ."

Juana spoke louder, for the man was undressing himself, oblivious to her words. He pulled her down on the bed beside her and gathered her in his arms.

"Please tell me if you've seen my father," Juana pleaded as she looked at his blind eye. "He had a rosary with him, a white rosary with heart-shaped beads."

The man stopped touching and looked at her. Juana breathed a sigh of relief, finally, he'd heard her.

"What did you say?" he asked.

"I said that I'm looking for my father, and that he had a white rosary with him."

The man scratched his head. Why did she feel that he knew something? Was it the way he avoided her eyes? The way he shook his head when she told him about the rosary?

"Please, señor, I need to find my father. I want to go home.

I'm so tired. So tired." The man got off the bed and walked around the hotel room pulling his hair, as if struggling against himself.

"His name's Miguel García. He's thirty-six years old, and he came from the state of Guerrero. He—"

The man put a hand up in the air, as if to stop her from talking. He dressed quickly, not bothering to button his shirt or tie his shoelaces. He looked at her. Juana looked at his blind eye, trying to find the truth hidden inside its darkness.

"Forgive me," he said. He stuffed his money into her hand and then turned around and left. Juana ran naked down the hallway.

"Please, señor, tell me what you know, tell me!"

The man stopped halfway down the stairs and turned around. "I know nothing," he said.

Juana watched him leave, certain that he had lied.

They celebrated Juana's fifteenth birthday by going to the beach in Puerto Nuevo. Adelina said they had the best lobster there for miles around. Juana didn't know what lobster was. Adelina had drawn a picture of it for her.

"It looks like a deformed roach," Juana said. And they had both shaken with laughter.

Adelina ordered an extra large lobster for them to share.

"A small one would do, Adelina. Just to taste what it's like," Juana said.

"No, no, Juana. You're a quinceañera today, and we must celebrate the right way."

So they stuffed themselves with lobster and rice, and when

they could eat no more, Adelina and Juana headed down to the beach. Juana stared at the water for a long time. She'd never seen the ocean before. And she had never thought she would ever see it. Her mother loved the ocean, too.

Amá had always wanted to see the ocean "in person." Juana could still remember that one time when they'd gone to the mercado, and they walked by the new travel agency. The agent was busy talking to his clients. Amá left Juana waiting outside, and she hesitantly walked inside the small office to look at the posters. Some posters were of sandy beaches and water shining a bright blue under the sun. In other posters the beaches were painted with the gold, orange, and red of the last rays of the sun. The silhouettes of palm trees framed the rolling waves in the distance.

A pile of travel magazines of beach resorts lay on a table nearby. With mouth agape and her eyes still glued on the posters, Amá accidentally bumped into the table, and the magazines splashed onto the floor like waves.

The travel agent looked up and coughed. Amá mumbled an apology and began to pick up all the magazines. When the agent turned back to his clients, Amá stuffed one magazine into her shopping bag and ran out of the office. Amá had never seen the ocean, and Juana wondered if she was afraid that one day she would find herself on her deathbed, in a town that was no more than three hours away from the Pacific Ocean, having never seen it.

Juana remembered how much Amá had prayed for forgiveness for having stolen the magazine. But at the same time, she couldn't help flipping through her beach resort magazine admiring the blue shimmering water of the sea.

But one rainy day when they didn't have coal, and the sticks Juana could have gathered outside were wet, Amá had kissed her magazine good-bye before burning it in the brazier. No one had enjoyed their meal that night.

Juana and Adelina sat down on the sand and listened to the crashing of the waves.

"I wish we could stay here forever, Juana," Adelina said as she closed her eyes.

Juana didn't answer. She knew that soon she would have to move on. She only wished she could take Adelina with her.

"Have you made a birthday wish?" Adelina asked.

Juana nodded. "I made a wish for the both of us."

"You did?"

"Yes. I wished that soon we will get to see our brothers again."

Adelina looked back at the sea and smiled. "That's a good birthday wish, Juana. Thank you."

adelina

Adelina was afraid to meet Sebastian's family. He invited her to his mother's house to celebrate her sixtieth birthday, and even though Adelina wanted to decline his invitation, she didn't. She had returned from Watsonville two days before and was in no mood to attend a party. But this was a special day for him, and she didn't want to ruin it. He hugged her so tenderly when she said she would come that she knew she couldn't back out.

They got to San Bernardino at dusk. His mother lived in a white house surrounded by a wooden picket fence. Rosebushes grew alongside the fence, and garden lights lit the walkway to the house. There were red, green, and blue balloons tied to the railing. As they waited for the door to be opened, Adelina breathed in the sweet scent of jasmine climbing on a trellis on the porch and struggled with the memories that scent evoked.

The door was opened.

"Sebastian!" said a tall young woman whose green eyes lit up upon seeing him. They embraced with Sebastian still holding Adelina's hand. It was as if he were afraid she would take off running. He was right. Adelina felt like doing just that.

"Jennifer, let me introduce you to Adelina. Adelina, this is my sister, Jennifer. She came down from Berkeley for the weekend."

Adelina shook Jennifer's hand. "It's a pleasure meeting you."

"It's great to meet you, too," Jennifer said as she leaned over to give Adelina a kiss on the cheek. "Come in, come in," Jennifer said as she ushered them inside.

The house was brimming with people, their words and laughter floating in the room above the music.

"Sebastian!"

"Mom!" Adelina turned around and saw a small gray-haired woman coming toward them, followed by four women slightly younger than she.

Sebastian rushed to her side, taking Adelina with him. He held her in a tight embrace. "Happy, happy birthday."

He introduced Adelina.

"I'm so pleased to meet the woman who has brought happiness to my son," Susana said.

"And these are my aunts: Carla, Norma, Leticia, and Gloria," Sebastian said.

"Nice to meet you," Adelina said, as she shook their hands.

"Hey, Sebastian, how's it going, man?"

"This is my cousin, Alfred," Sebastian said to Adelina as he shook a young man's hand.

Adelina smiled, but she felt the room spinning around her. More and more people came to say hello.

Finally, Sebastian led her to an empty seat in the living room.

"Let me get you a drink," he said. Adelina nodded, grateful for the chance to compose herself.

It wasn't long before Adelina was whisked off to the kitchen by Sebastian's mother, where she and her sisters were making tamales.

They stood around a large pot filled with dough. On the side were two bowls filled with green sauce and chile guajillo sauce. Another bowl was filled with shredded chicken meat and another with shredded pork meat. They talked about their husbands, children, and nieces and nephews as they made the tamales. So and so lost their first tooth, needed glasses, or had been accepted to some university.

Adelina picked up a wet cornhusk and lathered it with dough. Then she put shredded chicken and a spoonful of sauce in it before folding it and putting it inside a pot. She did what she saw these women do. She had never made tamales before.

"So what do you do for a living, Adelina?" one of the aunts asked.

"I'm a social worker. I work at a women's shelter in downtown L.A."

"Do you? You and Sebastian have many things in common then. He, too, likes to help others."

"And your parents, do they live with you in L.A?" another aunt asked.

"No," Adelina said.

Susana noticed Adelina's discomfort and said, "Come, come, mujeres. This was the last batch of tamales to be steamed. The other batch is done." She went around to Adelina's side. "Come mi'ja, let's get out of this kitchen and let them clean up this mess."

"Hey, where are you going?" Norma said.

"I'm the birthday girl," Susana said. "And Adelina is my guest. I think we're entitled to go mingle with the crowd. You four brujas clean up my kitchen, you hear?"

Adelina followed Susana to the living room where Sebastian was talking to his father and brother. He motioned for her to come, and Adelina rushed to his side and let his arm wrap around her.

Adelina excused herself and made her way to the bathroom where, on her way, she looked at the pictures hanging in the hallway. Picture frames of various shapes and sizes held images of Sebastian's family. There was a picture of a little boy showing off a gap-toothed smile whom she immediately recognized as Sebastian. She saw a picture of a younger version of Susana wrapped in the arms of her bearded husband. In another picture she saw a family portrait: Susana holding a little baby girl in her arms, her husband sitting beside her, and a teenage Sebastian and his younger brother standing on each side.

Adelina felt a twinge of jealousy. What wouldn't she give to have a picture like that of her family?

She was happy for Sebastian that he had such a family. He deserved happiness. After her recent trip to Watsonville, Adelina realized that happiness was something she couldn't give him. At least, not until she found her father.

"Here you are," Sebastian said as he came up behind her.

"We're going to cut the cake, Adelina. Come, let's go sing happy birthday." He put his arm around her waist and guided her out to the patio.

On the way home Adelina thought about her trip up north. Sebastian held her hand while he drove, as if trying to reassure her. He kept glancing at her from time to time, sensing that something was wrong. She wished she could tell him about the man she had hoped was her father. She wished she could tell him about the bus ride back from Watsonville, how she had cried for Miguel García and for herself. Neither of them had found what they were looking for.

"Promise me you'll try, Adelina," Don Ernesto had said.

Adelina looked out the car window. Miguel García had given himself a chance to be happy with Gloria. But Adelina knew she couldn't do the same.

She opened her mouth to speak, and broke the promise she'd made to Don Ernesto.

juana

Adelina wasn't home when Gerardo came. She'd been hired for the whole night by one of her regular clients. Juana didn't like for Adelina to stay out so late. She didn't want to chance being alone with Gerardo. Sure enough, sometime in the early hours of the morning, Juana succumbed to exhaustion. She woke up with a start when Gerardo, sitting on her bed, put his hand on her breasts. She sat up and pushed him away.

"Get away from me!"

"Come on, nena, there's no need to get feisty. You're a puta, remember? You like getting fucked. Tell me, how do you like it? Do you like it rough, like this?" Gerardo bit Juana's lips and twisted her hair around his fingers.

Juana cried out and pushed against him. "Leave me alone!"

"No, chiquita, I've been waiting too long for this moment. There's no way I'm going to let you go now." He got up and pulled down his pants. Juana scrambled out of bed, trying to head to the door, but Gerardo wrapped his arms tight around her. Juana bit his arm hard, tasting his blood in her mouth. She kicked and screamed for help, although she knew that none of the other girls would come to her aid.

"Puta!" Gerardo yelled, then threw her on the bed and pulled out his switchblade. Juana felt the blade against her throat. She felt her underwear being torn off. Gerardo pinned her against the bed, with her back to him. He clutched her wrists with one hand, and with the other buried her head in the pillow, and then thrust into her.

Juana wished the knife would cut her. She felt her vagina burning, felt him thrust inside her, hurting her again and again. She wanted to die, and yet, deep inside, she knew she had to survive. She made herself go limp, and tried not to think about the pain. She closed her eyes and thought about the rock, and the fields, and the river, and the blue sky all around her.

Gerardo climaxed and pushed her away from him. He stood in front of her and wiped the sweat off his forehead as he laughed. Juana stood up, feeling his semen sliding down her legs. She gathered saliva in her mouth and spat on his face.

Juana was packing her clothes into a backpack when Adelina came home. Adelina gasped when she saw her swollen eye and cut lip.

"Who did this to you?" Adelina asked.

Juana remained silent.

"Juana, talk to me, who did this? Was it a client?" Adelina sat down on a chair and looked at her.

"Gerardo," Juana said.

Adelina sat up, shaking her head. "No, Juana, he couldn't have."

"I'm leaving, Adelina."

"He didn't mean it, Juana. Maybe he was angry because he didn't find me here—"

"What are you saying?"

"I know Gerardo has a bad temper, and I make him angry all the time. I'm sure he didn't mean to hit you."

Juana remained quiet for a moment, wondering if she should tell Adelina the truth. Instead she said, "Come with me, Adelina. Let's leave all of this behind."

Adelina shook her head. "No, Juana. I can't leave. I can't."

"But why?"

"I-I love him."

Juana made a fist in the air. "But Adelina—"

"I know, you think I'm stupid, but that's how it is, Juana. I can't leave him."

Juana stood up. She pulled her T-shirt off and turned her back to Adelina. She heard Adelina gasp.

"Juana—"

"Those are Gerardo's bite marks," Juana said.

"But why would he do that?"

"He raped me, Adelina, don't you understand? That hijo de puta raped me!"

The room was quiet for a long time. Adelina went to lie in her bed and hugged her pillow against her chest. Juana continued putting her things inside her backpack. She didn't regret telling Adelina the truth, but at the same time, she hated herself for hurting her friend in that way.

Sometime later, Adelina finally stood up and went to her dresser. She pulled out a paper from the bottom drawer. Juana could see it from the corner of her eye. She knew what that paper was. It was Adelina's U.S. birth certificate.

"What about the blind man?" Adelina asked, breaking the silence.

"We've searched for weeks and have not found him," Juana said. "I can't keep wasting time looking for him. It's like he's hiding from me. I have to go to El Otro Lado and search for my father there."

Adelina nodded. She peeled off one of the pictures she'd taped on the dresser mirror and looked at it for a long time. It was the only picture she had of her family. Juana watched her trace the faces of her parents and brother with her fingertip. Adelina sighed and said, "All right, Juana, I'll go with you."

"Really, Adelina?" Juana went to stand beside Adelina.

"Yes, Juana. I think you're right. Maybe I don't belong here. Maybe there's still a chance for me."

Juana looked at their reflection in the dresser mirror and smiled.

There were only two women in the group that awaited the coyote, Juana and a small, dark-skinned woman in her thirties. The rest were all men. Four men with bulging veins in their arms, calluses in their hands, and lines of determination deeply etched into their foreheads. Juana looked at her reflection in the glass doors of the motel lobby. She saw her thin arms and small legs and wished she was bigger and stronger.

An old man sat behind the counter and looked nervously

at the clock. He was the motel's receptionist and the coyote's assistant. Earlier, he had given everyone in the group bottles of water, oranges, bread, dry cheese, a can of jalapeños, a small jar of mayonnaise, and a roll of toilet paper for the journey across the border. The clock read twelve-fifteen. Fifteen minutes more to wait.

Juana noticed that everyone was fidgety. The four men and the woman looked around the lobby, trying to avoid each other's eyes. They looked at the floor. At the ceiling. At their hands. They clutched the straps of their backpacks so tightly their knuckles were white. Juana was glad she was not the only one who was nervous and scared. She, too, was afraid of dying while attempting to cross the border. That was one of the many things she and Adelina had learned from all the coyotes they'd slept with. One never knew if they'd live to see El Otro Lado.

She was frightened, not because she was afraid of death, but because if she died, she would never again see her father.

Juana noticed that the woman was holding a rosary in her hands. It was barely noticeable, for the rosary beads were a dark shade of brown, almost the same color as the woman's hands. Juana could see the silver cross, and she could see the woman's lips moving in a silent prayer.

Juana wished she, too, had the courage to pray.

Suddenly, the door opened and everyone jumped, startled.

"Everyone's ready," the coyote's assistant said quickly.

A man dressed in jeans and a dark green shirt nodded at him and then looked at the group.

"Where's Octavio?" Juana asked. This was not the coyote

she and Adelina had paid to take her to the other side. Once she got across, she would call Adelina who would then join her in Chula Vista.

"He's sick," the coyote said. He turned to his assistant and asked, "Did you fill up their backpacks?"

The attendant nodded.

"Well, listen all of you, my name's Antonio. This is what we're going to do. I'm going to walk out this door and you'll follow behind me. But don't walk together. Maybe alone, or in pairs, and don't get too close to me. We'll go to the bus stop a few blocks from here and we'll catch the bus that'll take us to the terminal. Does everyone understand?"

Everyone nodded.

"All right, then let's go."

Juana stayed where she was, uncertain as to whether she should follow. She trusted Octavio. He was a regular client and she knew him to be honest and kind, which was unusual for a coyote. But she didn't know much about this coyote.

"Well, are you coming or not?" the coyote asked as he held the door opened for her.

Juana nodded, and made her way out the door.

The bus left Juana's group in the middle of deserted land. There was no fence on the side were they stood, but a chain-link fence ran along the other side of the road. Juana could see nothing but cacti and shrub for miles around.

"Well, this is where we begin," the coyote said as they crossed the road.

One by one they got through a hole in the fence.

"If any of you ever feel that you can't make it," the coyote said, looking at Juana and the woman, "tell me and I'll leave you somewhere where la migra can find you and take you back."

Juana looked at the expressionless faces of the four men, then she looked at the woman. The woman kissed the rosary she had in her hand and smiled at Juana.

"La Virgen will help us," she said.

Juana said nothing.

"You must keep up, señora," the coyote said to the woman. "And you," he said as he looked at Juana, "must do the same."

He turned around and the group followed silently behind him. The sun shone behind Juana's back, casting her shadow in front of her. Juana stepped on her shadow as she began her journey to El Otro Lado.

Juana felt as if they'd been going around in circles. She thought she could see the same cacti, the same shrubs, the same wild grass grasping her legs as she walked over them. How long had they been walking? Empty sandwich bags, cans of jalapeños, paper wrappings, bags of chips, soda cans, and plastic water bottles were scattered near shrubs and rocks, remnants of the people who came before her.

Here and there she could see clothing items hanging on shrubs, gently flapping in the wind, as if someone had done their wash and left it out to dry. Juana wondered why anyone would leave their clothes behind.

She raised her hand up to cover her eyes from the glare of the sun. Up in front of her, the coyote and the four men walked with sure, quick steps, as if they were impervious to the heat of the sun or the hunger pangs in their stomachs. It took a great effort for her legs to move, but Juana knew she had to keep up with them. She turned to glance back. The woman had fallen behind. She was dragging her feet forward, and she stooped to the ground, exhausted.

"Apúrese, señora," Juana said in a soft voice, she waved her hand and motioned for the woman to hurry.

The coyote stopped walking and told them it was time to eat. "But make it quick," he said, "we must keep going."

Juana sat on a rock and turned to look at the woman. She was still making her way toward them. When she finally arrived the men were already eating their bread and cheese. Juana was sipping on her tepid water.

"Señora," the coyote said. "Maybe it would be best if you stay here and wait for la migra to come. You're putting us in danger of being caught."

The woman shook her head. "No, señor, please don't leave me behind. I can make it. Slowly, but I can make it."

The coyote shook his head. "I don't know. I don't think you can."

The woman sat next to Juana and took an orange from her backpack. She looked at Juana timidly, and tried to smile.

"I'm Lourdes," she said. "What's your name?"

"Juana."

"I have to get to the other side," she said.

Juana nodded.

"My children need me. I must get back to them."

"Were you deported?" Juana asked.

"Yes. I started working at a restaurant, cleaning and washing dishes. A week later, the day I was to be paid, I showed up to work and la migra arrived and took some of us away. Too late I found out that the boss called la migra on us so he wouldn't have to pay us."

"I'm sorry," Juana said.

Lourdes nodded. "I need to get back to my children."

"Well, if anyone needs to use the restroom, now is a good time to go," the coyote said.

The men headed toward a pile of rocks. Juana and Lourdes headed in the opposite direction, to a cluster of shrubs close by. Juana took her roll of toilet paper along. As she relieved herself she looked around her, keeping an eye out for snakes, coyotes, or tarantulas. There was a familiar smell drifting toward her. The smell of a dead animal.

Suddenly, Lourdes started screaming.

Juana scrambled to her feet and ran to where she was. Lourdes stood rooted to the ground, screaming and pointing at something in the shrubs.

"What's going on? What's going on?" the men asked as they came running.

"Shut up, mujer," the coyote said, "la migra might hear us!"

Juana pulled Lourdes against her and tried to calm her. A dead man lay on the ground a few meters away from them.

Juana could see his pale skin and a huge bump on his forehead. His eyes were shut, his face relaxed as if in a deep sleep. Juana wished she could go scare off the flies buzzing all around him.

"Poor bato," the coyote said, "He probably didn't even know what hit him."

"Who do you think did it?" one of the men asked.

"His coyote, probably," the coyote said. He laughed when he saw the men looking at him, with fear in their eyes. "Hey, some coyotes do that, you know. But they aren't real coyotes. They just lie to people and bring them here, where they can kill them and take their money. But trust me, I won't do that."

Juana told herself that when the group began to move she would purposefully walk behind him. She wasn't going to take any chances.

When the coyote said it was time to continue, he told Juana and Lourdes they would go first, alone.

"But why?" Juana asked. "We have to stay with you. You're the one who knows where we're heading."

The coyote pointed to an antenna in the distance. "That's where we're heading. Try to hide among the bushes, and stay low. We'll catch up to you soon enough."

"But—"

"Look, Juana, that's how it's going to be. You two are slowing us down. So we'll give you a head start. The men and I will stay here and rest a little longer, and you and la señora must start walking. Or you can stay here and wait for la migra."

Juana looked at Lourdes.

"Let's go," Lourdes said. "We'll show them what we're made of."

Juana forced herself to stand up, put on her backpack, and begin to walk. They were being sent out as bait for la migra. She knew that if she and Lourdes were caught, the coyote and the four men would have a chance to flee.

• • •

The sun had gone down and now darkness was spreading all around them, but still, Juana could clearly see five men walking toward them.

"Do you really think it's them?" Lourdes asked.

Juana nodded.

"We must thank La Virgen de Guadalupe for Her help," Lourdes said as she crossed herself. Juana stood up from among the bushes and waited for the men to get to where she stood.

"Hey, glad you made it safely," the coyote said to Juana. She nodded, noticing the look of surprise in his face. Was he disappointed?

"Well, let's sit down and rest," the coyote said. Juana was glad he didn't say they must continue. She and Lourdes had only arrived ten minutes ago to this spot, and they were tired, having walked fast trying to stay ahead of the men. There had been many times when Juana felt they would not make it.

"How much longer will it be?" one of the men asked.

"We won't get there till tomorrow, Pancho," the coyote said. "We're going slow. Too slow sometimes."

The moon was like a bright peso cut in half. Farther up ahead, on a hill, Juana could see little red lights shining in the darkness. Like evil eyes looking down at her. She shivered.

"What's that?" she asked the coyote.

"Antennas."

Not since Juana left her hometown had she walked this much. She kept looking at the evil red eyes of the antennas. They didn't seem to be getting closer.

She heard a growling sound, and for a moment she thought it was her stomach. But the coyote suddenly stopped walking and told everyone to stop. They stood and listened. Juana held her breath.

That sound again, getting closer.

"Helicopter," the coyote said. "Quick, find somewhere to hide!" They followed after him, jumping over rocks and shrubs. A dry branch grabbed Juana's arm and tore a hole in her sweater.

"Hurry, hurry!"

Juana kept running through the darkness.

"Juana!"

She turned around and could barely see Lourdes lying on the ground.

She ran back and picked her up, and when they turned around the men had been swallowed up by the darkness. The helicopter came into view now, the noise chopping the silence. A bright light shone above, searching.

"Where are they? Where are they?" Lourdes asked.

"Let's go!" Juana said, as she pulled her along. They ran and ran, away from the light and the noise.

"Hurry!"

There was nowhere to hide. Juana and Lourdes blindly ran through the shrubs, their sharp branches clutching at them, as if trying to trap them. The branches scratched Juana's arms and face, but still she kept running.

"Psssst. Over here. Over here."

They followed the sound of the voice and found a cluster of shrubs that had grown so close together they had formed a small cave.

"Over here."

Something white was waving in the darkness, and Juana led Lourdes to it.

"Get inside, hurry!"

Juana closed her eyes, held her breath, and listened. The helicopter was roaring above them, its light like a sword cutting through the darkness.

Lourdes's fingers squeezed Juana's arm tightly. "Please, Virgencita, please save us, don't let them find us, don't—"

"Calm down, señora," Juana whispered. But Lourdes continued mumbling, and she clutched Juana's arm even tighter.

Light fell over a man's face, and Juana recognized Julio, one of the men in their group. As the "cave" grew dark again, Juana could no longer see his face, but she could still see his eyes in her mind, big round eyes opened wide with fear.

They walked alongside a dirt road. Once in a while Juana could see the road through the shrubs. The coyote said it was unsafe to walk on the road, so instead they had to walk through the bushes, staying close to the ground. Her legs ached, and her eyes were heavy with sleep. What kept her awake was the cold night air and the sharp, painful fear buried deep within her stomach.

"Listen, la migra is coming," the coyote whispered. "Drop to the ground. Quick!"

They instantly dropped and hid behind the shrubs. The purring of an engine got louder. Soon, a large white truck passed by on the dirt road.

Keep going, keep going, please, Juana thought.

The truck stopped farther down the road, not too far from where they were. Juana realized with dismay that it wasn't going to go anywhere.

"Shit. We're too late," the coyote said.

"For what?" Eugenio asked.

"For the change in shifts. There's always a gap between shifts when there's no one here, but we got here too late. We can't sit here for hours and wait for the next shift."

"And we're too many. They'll see us for sure," Pancho said.

The coyote was quiet for a moment, thinking, then he said, "Listen up. We're going to split up into two groups. Roberto, Eugenio, and Pancho come with me. You two women go with Julio."

"But—"

"Now listen, Julio, I can't have all seven of us try to get past la migra together. We'll get caught for sure. It's better this way. Us four, and you three. Now, do you see the hill over there?"

Juana turned to look at the silhouette of the hill rising on the other side of la migra.

"Yes, I see it," Julio said.

"All right, that's where we're going to meet. You take your group down the road and try to get past. And I'll take my group around this hill here."

"Pero, señor, I want to stay with you," Lourdes said. "I need to make sure I get to the other side. I have to get back to Los Angeles."

"Señora, this hill is full of loose dirt and rocks, and I don't want you falling. You follow the path, and keep an eye out for la migra. We'll meet over there."

Pancho, Roberto, Eugenio, and the coyote disappeared into the shrubs.

Juana's group was left standing in the darkness. The three looked toward the road where, a few meters away, la migra was waiting.

They took turns moving. Julio said it must be done that way because if they all moved at the same time they would make too much noise. Lourdes went first. She moved quietly through the shrubs, walking on her toes in small steps. When she got to a rock she crouched low and waited. Juana went next. For the first time, she was glad she was small and thin, for she made no noise when she walked toward the rock where Lourdes was. She, too, crouched low and waited. Julio was last. He was big and clumsy, but he managed to be quiet enough.

They moved slowly a few meters at a time, crouching behind rocks or shrubs. When they finally got to the place where la migra was parked, they moved even more carefully, for even the smallest noise could give them away. Juana held her breath as she moved. When it was Lourdes's turn, she tripped over a rock and grabbed the branches of a nearby shrub to keep her balance. But the branches broke and Lourdes fell to the ground.

The thud was loud against the silence. They all held their breath and waited. Juana could see the two immigration officers talking, but she couldn't make out what they were saying. One of them threw his cigarette on the ground and crushed it with his heel, then the two of them walked toward the noise, toward Juana.

She heard their footsteps getting closer. They pushed the branches of the shrubs to the side and walked toward her, getting closer and closer. Lourdes didn't move. She sat on the ground, biting her hand to keep from crying out.

Something ran out of the bushes near where Julio was hiding.

"Whoa!" the officers said, surprised.

An animal jumped over a rock and then scurried away, back into the darkness.

"It's just a fox," one of them said.

The immigration officers moved away, back to their truck.

"Do you see that over there?" the coyote asked. "That's an American road—we're almost there."

El Otro Lado! Juana breathed a sigh of relief. They sat on top of the hill, resting after the long walk. She was almost there. Soon, she and Adelina would be together again.

"Now what we are going to do is run," the coyote said, "run as fast as you can. You're going to come up to a fence. It's just three metal wires running across. You must not touch the wires. They have sensors. So if you move them they'll transmit that movement to la migra, who will come here and take a look. Now, let's go."

Juana needed no more prompting. She took off and ran, ran, ran as fast as she could, trying to keep up with the men. Her sides began to burn, her lungs screamed for air, but she didn't stop until she was at the fence. She followed the men and crawled through the gaps between the wires and passed through to the other side.

"Welcome to the United States," the coyote said.

Juana took deep gulps of air. American air.

They walked underneath a row of cables suspended on the towers the coyote said they must guide themselves by. The towers made a loud buzzing sound, like thousands of swarming bees.

As they walked on a trail in single file, Juana wondered if her father had come this way. There was a point where the trail led them under a tower. As they walked underneath its metal skeleton Juana felt that at any minute, it could come crashing down on top of them. The earth rumbled under her feet. She could almost feel the energy transported in the cables. The buzzing was loud, vibrating inside her skull. She walked faster.

It was dawn when they got to the last tower. In front of them was what looked like a dry river.

"Everyone stay on the rocks. Don't step on the sand," the coyote said. "You might leave footprints that la migra could follow." Several minutes later, the coyote stopped walking. "Okay, everyone, this is it."

Juana looked around, uncertain as to what he meant. All around them were huge boulders, like giants towering above on either side. It reminded Juana of a tale Doña Martina once told her, about giant rocks that whistle. She wondered if this was how they looked. The coyote pointed at the crevices and said that was where they'd sleep.

"We should have gotten here at three," he said.

It was now seven in the morning. The sun was already shining above.

They all had to crawl into the crevices, for they were too small for them to be able to sit up. Juana didn't mind. When they were all lying down, the coyote walked around and handed everyone bread and cheese. Juana ate quickly. She rested her head over her arms and closed her eyes for a long-awaited sleep.

At three in the afternoon the group began to walk again. After an hour of walking they finally got to a paved road.

"We need to get to the other side of that road," the coyote said. "Someone is waiting there for us in a car. But there's la pinche migra again, parked farther down. It's too dangerous to run across the road. We have to keep walking."

So they walked for another half hour until they got to a tunnel. The tunnel was dark and wet. It smelled like rotten water and dead animals. They had to go through it on their hands and knees. The ridges on the metal dug into Juana's knees, which after a few minutes, were swollen with pain. It was so dark she felt as if she had her eyes shut tight. She blinked over and over again, to find no relief from this absence of light.

She wasn't sure where the others were. They had started off together, the coyote ahead of them, Pancho and Roberto behind him. She couldn't hear them in front. But behind her were Julio, Eugenio, and Lourdes moaning in pain.

When she finally got to the other side, it was the bright light she had to adjust to. She kept her eyes closed for a few seconds until they stopped hurting. When she opened her eyes,

Roberto, Pancho, and the coyote were sitting on the ground, staring at her. Three gringos dressed in green uniforms stood behind them.

"How many more are there?" one of them asked the coyote.

"Three," the coyote said.

Juana turned around and dove back into the tunnel. She had to get away from them. She had come so far now. Someone grabbed her legs and she kicked as hard as she could. She dug her fingernails into the metal and scraped it, trying to hold on.

adelina

Adelina walked into the hospital room Dr. Schaffer took her to, and closed the door softly behind her. Diana turned and looked but didn't smile or make any attempt to acknowledge Adelina's presence. She turned back to look at the television hanging on the wall.

Adelina pulled up a seat beside Diana's bed. She glanced at Diana's wrists. They were covered with white bandages.

"How are you feeling?" she asked as she sat down.

Diana didn't look away from the TV.

Adelina reached down to touch Diana's hand, careful not to hurt her.

"You should have just left me there," Diana said.

"Diana—"

"I want to die, Adelina. I can't live like this, with this pain that chokes me up inside until I can't breathe."

"Pain takes time to heal, Diana. One day you will not hurt the way you're hurting now."

Diana snorted. She turned to look at Adelina and said, "What do you know about pain? You don't know what it's like to be responsible for a child's death. You don't know what it's like for me when night comes, when my body yearns for rest and my guilty conscience can't let it sleep."

Adelina fought back the tears gathering in her eyes. She hated crying. It was a rare thing for her to cry, because unlike other people, who feel better when they cry, Adelina felt much worse.

"You don't know what it's like, Adelina, to stay awake at night, fighting the demons who haunt you, who don't let you sleep."

Adelina wiped the tear running down her cheek. She took a deep breath and said, "Yes, I do. Let me tell you a story, Diana. The story of a young girl who fell asleep one rainy night and drowned her sister."

juana

Juana flicked on the light and walked into the room. She threw her backpack down on her bed and sat down. It was eight in the evening. Adelina was supposed to be here, waiting for her phone call. She had not answered the phone earlier when Juana, once released by la migra, had called. She was afraid Adelina had changed her mind.

She walked to Adelina's bed and picked up the blankets. She had thought she was just imagining things, but the red stains on the blankets were real. Juana held the blankets closer to the light, then tossed them down and ran out of the room. She ran downstairs and banged on Veronica's door. No one answered. Juana kept knocking. She knew that Veronica always brought her clients to her apartment. She said she hated hotel rooms and preferred instead to work in the comfort of her own home.

"Veronica, it's Juana. Please open the door!"

The door swung open and Veronica stood there, wrapped

in a blanket. Juana saw the stranger lying in the bed, upset at being interrupted.

"Veronica, do you know what happened to Adelina?"

Veronica opened her mouth to speak, but was interrupted by the man in the bed.

"Hurry up, bitch, I'm getting soft."

Veronica stepped out of her room and closed the door behind her. She pulled Juana to the side.

"I came home and found her blankets stained with blood," Juana said quickly. "Please, tell me—"

"I'm sorry, Juana."

"Where is she? Is she okay?"

Veronica shook her head. "She's dead. Gerardo killed her. That son of a bitch killed her!"

Something hit the door from the inside, and Juana could hear the man yelling for Veronica to get back to work.

Veronica opened the door to her room.

"She told him she was leaving him. I'm sorry, Juana. I-I called the ambulance, but they got here too late." Veronica closed the door softly behind her.

Juana headed back upstairs. She sat on her bed and felt her body shudder. She felt that a part of her had just died as well.

She picked up her backpack and hung it on her shoulder. She had to get out of here. She couldn't stay here anymore. She went to the dresser and peeled off the pictures she and Adelina had taped there. Pictures of them together. She opened the bottom drawer and took out Adelina's birth certificate. Juana looked at it for a long time, memorizing the information recorded there. She looked at her reflection in the mirror and opened her mouth to speak.

"What's your name?" she asked herself in English, knowing that was the first question immigration officials would ask.

"My name's Adelina. Adelina Vasquez."

Juana switched off the light, closed the door behind her, and made her way to the border inspection station.

adelina

The taxicab ambled along the dirt road that ran parallel to the river, heading north. It made its way over potholes and small rocks. Most of the shacks made of bamboo sticks and cardboard had become concrete houses. Adelina stared at the tiny shack that had once belonged to Doña Martina, and wondered who lived there now. She saw a little naked boy running around outside the shack chasing away the chickens and ducks his mother was trying to feed.

Adelina saw the vacant lot in the distance. Boys and girls were playing soccer. She watched as one girl raised her leg up and kicked the soccer ball high into the air. A cloud of dust rose from the place where she'd kicked, the pebbles sprinkled down like raindrops. Adelina felt a twinge of jealousy, remembering how much she had once wished to play soccer with the boys.

The taxicab came to a stop where her shack should have been.

Now a yellow brick and concrete house stood there, surrounded by a small brick wall to keep the river waters out during the floods. This was the house her father had once dreamed of.

Now it belonged to another.

"Let me help you with your luggage, señorita."

Adelina nodded, picked up the wooden box from the seat next to her, and got out of the cab. The door of the house opened and a short, plump woman came out. Two teenage boys and a small girl trailed behind her.

Adelina smiled. "Good afternoon, Sandra," she said to Doña Martina's granddaughter.

"I'm so glad you got here safely," Sandra said as she opened her arms to hug Adelina.

"It's nice to see you again," Adelina said, remembering that the last time she had seen Sandra was at the train station before she left for Tijuana.

Sandra told the oldest boy to take the luggage in and led Adelina into the house.

The concrete walls were painted a light shade of blue. The sunlight was streaming through the large open windows. Adelina looked down at the concrete floor.

"Are you sorry the shack's gone, Juana?" Sandra asked.

Adelina looked at her, surprised to be called by her real name.

"I'm sorry," Sandra said, "I should call you Adelina."

"Adelina died a long time ago. Maybe it's time to let her rest. You should call me Juana. That's who I am."

Sandra motioned for Adelina to sit on the couch.

"I think you're wrong," Sandra said. "You aren't Juana anymore. You're now a successful woman who has done what needed to be done. You should keep your new name—Adelina."

She had always felt guilty about using the real Adelina's birth certificate to cross the border, go to college, and get a job.

Sandra looked at the wooden box Adelina had placed next to her on the couch.

"My father's ashes," she said. "Sandra, how is my mother?"

"She's doing better. The doctor was able to fight the infection in her lungs, thank God."

"Has she started eating again?"

"No."

"How long has she been doing this?" Adelina asked as she opened her purse. She took out the white rosary and began to rub the beads with her fingers.

"Almost three weeks."

Adelina shook her head. What was Amá trying to do?

"She's so frail now. She looks like a very old woman, but she's only fifty-one. She's becoming delusional. Keeps talking to the wall as if she sees your father there. Sometimes she rocks her arms back and forth as if she were holding a baby."

"When can we go see her?"

"Visiting hours are in the morning. I'll take you to your mother tomorrow."

Later in the afternoon, Adelina excused herself and made her way to the other side of the river to catch a taxicab to the town square. She decided to go for a stroll around the plaza. She would have preferred to go sit on her rock, but she knew that once alone, she would remember things she didn't want to, feel things she didn't want to.

She would think of Sebastian.

Adelina got out of the taxicab and crossed the street to the plaza. Her long peasant skirt flapped around her in the afternoon breeze. She looked up at the tamarind trees around the plaza swaying gently in the wind. She sat on a bench and watched the couples who were strolling hand in hand, the children running up and down the steps of the monument, where a large Mexican flag flapped on a pole. She looked at the clusters of men who were laughing together, their eyes looking hungrily at the pretty girls giggling behind cupped hands.

Vendors lined the streets, some selling corn on the cob, pancakes with syrup or jam, fried plantains, churros, or mangoes on a stick. Adelina felt her mouth water as she breathed in the smell of corn. Amá had once loved corn.

"Good afternoon, señorita."

Adelina looked up and was startled to see the young man with the droopy eyes, the man she now knew was her eighteen-year-old brother. He stood in front of her. Doña Matilde clung to his right arm, looking at her.

Adelina looked at the old woman, feeling all the hatred of old engulf her.

She took a deep breath and tried to steady herself. "Good afternoon, joven. It is such a surprise to see you again," she heard herself say.

Her brother laughed. Adelina winced. It was her father's laugh.

"I'm not surprised to see you. This is a very small town, after all. You ran away from the bus station so quickly you didn't give me a chance to introduce my mother to you, Señora Matilde."

Doña Matilde stretched out her frail wrinkled hand to Adelina.

Adelina stood up, feeling herself empowered by the fact that she now towered over Doña Matilde's hunched figure. She looked down at the old woman's eyes, reached out to shake her hand, and said, "Good afternoon, señora. I'm Juana García."

Doña Matilde's eyes widened. Her lower jaw trembled. Her hand released Adelina's as if she had been burned.

"Mamá, aren't you going to say something?" her brother asked.

Doña Matilde looked down at the ground and didn't answer.

"Juana, please excuse my mother. But I'm sure she's very pleased to meet you. I'm José Alberto Díaz."

Adelina shook her brother's smooth hand. His was not the hand of a peasant, but that of a university student.

"Well, señorita, it was nice meeting you," Doña Matilde told Adelina through clenched teeth. She turned to José Alberto and said, "Mi'jo, it's getting chilly. Please let's go home."

"But you just said you wanted me to buy you a churro. Come, Mamá, wait here with Juana while I get it for you."

"But I—"

"Come, come, Mamá, you need to rest a minute." José Alberto gently helped Doña Matilde to sit down next to Adelina. Doña Matilde glared at her and moved to the other end of the bench, as far away from her as she could.

José Alberto turned to Adelina and excused himself. She watched him walk across the street. For a moment she thought about calling him back.

"What do you think you're doing?" Doña Matilde said.

Adelina turned to look at her. "I don't know what you mean, señora."

"You know exactly what I mean. I know who you are. You've been gone for years, and now you've come back to try to take my son from me. I can see that right away."

"He's not your son. He's my mother's child. My brother. And you stole him."

"He belonged to me. He's the child I should've had—"

Adelina got to her feet and pointed an accusatory finger at Doña Matilde. "But you didn't have him, my mother did."

"He's my son," Doña Matilde said. She pressed her cane to her chest, her wrinkled hands trembling. Adelina turned around and saw José Alberto heading toward them, carrying a churro in each hand.

"He's my mother's son and my brother," Adelina said, "and it's time we claimed him."

"You stay away from him," Doña Matilde whispered. "Or you're going to cause him a pain so great it'll haunt him for the rest of his life."

Adelina didn't take her eyes off José Alberto as he came up to them.

"Here you go. They're still hot," José Alberto said as he handed a churro to each.

Adelina looked at his boyish smile, his unruly hair, the carefree look in his eyes.

She thought about what Doña Matilde had said. She took a bite out of her churro, but the sugar didn't replace the bitterness in her mouth.

The bus ride to the Chilpancingo prison took more than an hour, but Adelina felt that they had gotten there quickly. Amá was in the prison's clinic. She was transferred back there a week ago, when the judiciales realized she was serious about starving herself to death.

She only had eight more years of her sentence left, but she'd given up and decided to die.

Adelina tightened her hold on the wooden box she carried in her arms. The judicial walking in front of her guided her out of the waiting area down a hallway.

With every step she took, Adelina felt her apprehension growing. She was afraid of seeing Amá now. She wanted to remember her mother the way she had looked years ago.

As she crossed the threshold, Adelina looked at the guards inside the small clinic. They stood ten feet apart, holding rifles in their hands. There were two rows of hospital beds on each side of the opposite walls. Screens stood between each bed, to allow for privacy.

"Come this way, please," the judicial told Adelina. They walked down the aisle. She kept her eyes looking forward, trying not to look at the other female prisoners lying on the beds.

The judicial came to a stop and pointed at the bed in front of him. "You have twenty minutes, señorita," he said.

The screen blocked Adelina's view. She took a few steps forward. Amá was looking at her, but there was no recognition in her eyes. Amá's small wrinkled hands peeked from the hospital sheet. There was an IV in her wrist. Adelina closed her eyes and tried to recall the times when she brushed her mother's long hair, when she cleaned the dirt off her mother's beautiful face, when she held her mother's hand in her own, when she breathed in the scent of jasmine that always enveloped Amá.

"Hello, Amá," she said, eyes opened. "It's me, Juana. Your daughter."

Amá looked at her and shook her head. "You aren't my Juana. No, my Juana is a young girl. She's a very smart girl, and she loves me very much. But she never comes to see me."

Adelina approached her mother and leaned down to kiss her forehead. She pulled up a chair beside the bed and sat down. She placed the wooden box on her lap, then reached out and grabbed Amá's hand.

"I know you," Amá said. "At least I think I know you. You look familiar, but I can't remember where I've seen you."

"Amá, I'm Juana. Your daughter." Adelina clutched her mother's hand tight.

She wanted so desperately for her mother to see her, to see Juana.

"Do you hear that, Miguel?" Amá said to the screen on

her right. "She says she's our Juana. But how can she be our Juana? She's so tall and pretty, and our Juana is still a shy young girl."

Adelina put her head down on her mother's lap, and without being able to control herself, she allowed the tears to come out. She wanted to be her mother's daughter again, not a stranger.

"There, there, child. There, there. There's no need for tears." Amá gently raised Adelina's head and dried her tears with the corner of the sheet. "All right, you can be my Juana, if you like," she said.

Adelina nodded.

"So why haven't you come to visit me before, Juana?" Amá asked.

"I was away. I was living in El Otro Lado."

Amá was quiet for a moment. She pressed her lips together, and Adelina saw her eyes become glossy with tears. "My husband is in El Otro Lado," she whispered. "Soon he will come back. He told me so. Soon we will be together." She turned back to the screen and said, "Verdad, Miguel? You'll be coming back to be with me. Verdad? Soon you will come back to me."

Adelina looked at the screen, almost expecting to see her father standing there, too.

Amá struggled to pull her knees up and hug them. She rocked herself back and forth, mumbling that Apá would soon come back.

"He left so long ago," Amá said. "But he'll come back. He promised he would come back for me." She turned to look at

Adelina and grabbed her hand. "He didn't lie to me, did he? He didn't abandon me?"

Adelina touched her mother's cheek. "No, Amá, Apá never abandoned you."

Amá smiled and wiped her eyes.

"Está bién, señorita, your time's up." The judicial stood behind Adelina and motioned for her to get up.

Adelina nodded, picked up the wooden box from her lap, and bent down to kiss her mother's forehead again.

"I'll come visit you tomorrow," she told her.

Amá nodded and laughed the carefree laugh of a young girl. She lowered her head, pressed her knees closer to her, and began to rock herself again.

"He didn't abandon me. He didn't abandon me . . ."

Adelina looked at her mother one more time before she allowed herself to be guided back out of the clinic, to the waiting area where Sandra was waiting for her.

She pressed the wooden box against her chest. She couldn't tell Amá that he was dead.

Amá wanted her husband back, not his ashes.

Adelina leaned against her rock and looked at the town below. The town had grown. She could see tiny lights glowing at the foot of the mountains. There had been no houses there before. She wrapped her sweater tighter, and felt the chilly wind in her hair.

It was five o'clock in the evening in L.A. Dinner was being prepared now at the shelter. She would have been driving down Fourth Street, heading west toward downtown, on her way to the shelter. She would be driving over the bridge, turning to look to the right where in the distance the General Hospital could be seen. And she would think of Sebastian working there, saving someone's life.

It hurt to think about him. The only man she had ever fallen in love with.

"What are you going to do about your father?" Sandra asked her the next morning as they embroidered servilletas. Sandra was trying to teach Adelina how to make different stitches with the needle. Adelina pricked her thumb and put it inside her mouth. It had been too many years since she'd embroidered.

"I'm not going to tell her anything," she told Sandra. "Amá won't accept my father's death. But there is one person who's still alive I can bring to her."

"What do you mean?" Sandra held the needle halfway between her face and the napkin and waited for Adelina to answer. Her eyebrows drew together in a frown.

Adelina looked at her and said, "Tomorrow when I visit Amá, I'm going to take my brother with me."

"Are you going to tell him the truth then?"

Adelina inserted the needle into the cloth and pulled out the long strand of shiny blue thread from the other side.

"He's my brother, Sandra. He's my mother's son. Yes, I will tell him the truth. Doña Matilde doesn't deserve his love, and I'm going to take it from her."

Sandra lay the napkin on the table. "Think about what it is that you're going to do, Adelina. Sometimes it's best to leave things alone. Your brother is a young man now. Whether you like it or not, Matilde has raised him well. She's given him all the love a mother could give.

"Sometimes it's best to walk away. If you do this out of revenge, be aware that you'll hurt not only Matilde but your brother and yourself, as well."

Adelina looked down at the needle she held in her hand. She wanted to tell José Alberto the truth. He was her brother. Wouldn't it be a relief to remove the weight she carried on her back, to share her pain, her worries, and the truth with the only member of her family who was still alive?

He was her brother. Would she have to lose him, too?

Adelina asked the taxicab driver to stop in front of Doña Matilde's house. She stood outside the black gate, looking at herself reflected on the metal sheet. She took a deep breath and knocked.

She didn't have to wait long. To her relief, José Alberto was the one who opened the gate. He was covered in dirt and sweat, and he wore a straw hat on his head.

"Juana, what a surprise. Come in, come in."

Adelina had never been inside Don Elías's house. Various types of plants adorned the path that led to the front door. Rose-bushes grew alongside the walls dividing the property from the people next door. Empty clay flowerpots were on the ground next to a bag of garden soil and geraniums ready to be potted.

"I'm fixing up my mother's garden," José Alberto said as he wiped the sweat from his forehead. "I just finished pruning the rosebushes and now I'm repotting some plants."

"I'm sorry I interrupted your work," Adelina said, swallowing the taste of jealousy in her mouth.

"No, you're not interrupting. Come, have a seat while I go get you a glass of lemonade." José Alberto led Adelina to the patio chairs on the porch. Adelina sat down, wondering where Doña Matilde was. When José Alberto came back out with two glasses of lemonade she asked him about Doña Matilde's whereabouts.

"She went to Mass. She'll be coming home soon. How did you know where I lived?" José Alberto asked.

Adelina took a drink. This was the time to tell him. She could tell him all about Don Elías, about what Doña Matilde did to Amá, about Amá being in prison, Apá dying, and about her going to look for him. But when she opened her mouth she couldn't bring herself to tell him. "I, ah, the taxicab driver knew where you lived."

"Yes, it's a small town." José Alberto said.

"I came to ask a favor of you."

"What is it?"

Adelina tapped her glass with her fingers, thinking about how to say what she wanted to say. "I need you to come with me to Chilpancingo. My mother is dying, and I would like for you to meet her."

José Alberto was quiet. Adelina wondered what he was thinking. Surely he was surprised. He had only met her yesterday, after all, and here she was making such a request. But she wanted him to see Amá first, before she told him the truth. She wanted to see how he would react upon seeing their mother.

"What's the matter with her?" José Alberto asked.

"She's been locked up in prison for seventeen years now. She's stopped eating, she's become delusional. Her mind has regressed to the past, to the point where she doesn't even know who I am."

"I'm so sorry to hear that," José Alberto said. Adelina looked at his tear-shaped eyes. When he smiled at her it was as if she was seeing Apá.

Just then the gate opened and Doña Matilde walked in, wrapped in a black shawl. She looked at José Alberto and Adelina.

"What's that woman doing here?" she said. Her cane shook in front of her, and she would have fallen if José Alberto had not run to her side to hold her steady.

"It's okay, Mamá, come and sit down," José Alberto said.

Doña Matilde shook her head and pointed a finger at Adelina. "I told you to stay away from him. I told you. What do you want from him? Do you want to ruin his life?"

"Mamá, that's enough. What's gotten into you?"

Adelina came to stand beside José Alberto, her heart pounding. *Tell him, tell him*, she told herself. *Tell him now.*

"My mother is dying, señora," Adelina said.

Doña Matilde shook her head and leaned against José Alberto. "Don't take him away, please, don't take him away."

José Alberto wrapped his arms around her and tried to calm her. "It's okay, Mamá, I'm here. It's okay."

Adelina let her arms drop to the sides. She looked at José Alberto. She heard the tenderness in his voice, saw the way he held Doña Matilde in his arms. Part of her wanted to tell him.

She wanted him to know his real mother. She wanted him to know who his father was. Who she was. But what would be gained by telling him the truth? Could he love Amá the way he loved Doña Matilde? Could he love the memory of a father he never met?

And could he love her, the sister he never knew he had?

She looked at her brother one more time, then turned to go.

"Wait!" José Alberto said. Adelina stopped walking, her hand on the gate handle. "I'll go with you tomorrow."

"José Alberto, mi'jo. Don't leave me," Doña Matilde said.

"Señora," Adelina said as she turned around to look at Doña Matilde, "my mother is dying." *And you owe it to her,* she wanted to say. But it seemed there was no need to say it aloud.

Doña Matilde had heard those silent words, for after a moment she nodded and said, "Then you must go, José Alberto. Go see that poor woman. Perhaps you can help her die in peace."

During the bus ride to Chilpancingo, Adelina kept waiting for José Alberto to ask why she had invited him along. He didn't. He was quiet for the most part. He had a faraway look in his eyes, deep in thought, as if he were trying to remember something and couldn't.

But then, Adelina thought, maybe he was just worried about Doña Matilde.

It would be so much easier to tell José Alberto the truth if Doña Matilde had mistreated him, or not loved him the way she did. If she told him now, he would probably hate Adelina for ruining the love he felt for the woman he thought was his mother.

"Where's your father, Juana?"

It took Adelina a moment to realize that José Alberto had spoken to her.

"My father died many years ago," she told him.

He looked surprised. "When? And how?"

"He died nineteen years ago, when he tried to cross the border to the United States. My mother and I didn't know about his death. I've only learned of it recently." Adelina turned to look at José Alberto and said, "My mother doesn't know. Please, don't mention it when you see her."

"Why don't you want her to know the truth?"

"Because she won't accept it. I once thought that if she knew my father had died and not abandoned her, she would be able to live in peace. But I was wrong. Telling her about my father's death would send her deeper into her depression. It would kill the hope she has kept alive all these years—that one day he will come back to her."

"It must have been hard for her to lose her husband," José Alberto said.

"Yes, it was." Adelina looked out the window and wiped away the moisture in her eyes.

"My mother lost her husband, too," José Alberto said. "She took it very hard. She rarely talks about him."

Why would she want to talk about that miserable bastard? Adelina thought.

"When I was younger I used to wish I had known my father. But one day I stopped wishing for that."

"Why?"

"When I looked at his pictures I felt as if I was looking at a stranger, at a person who was not a good man. And sometimes when people in the town would talk about him, they wouldn't say nice things."

"I understand why you felt that way," Adelina said.

"But the strange thing is that years ago our cleaning lady told me that he wasn't my father," José Alberto turned to look at Adelina. She held her breath and waited to hear more. Who was the cleaning lady? Why had she told José Alberto such a thing? How did she know?

"My mother overheard our conversation and fired her right then and there. When she was leaving she started yelling things that didn't make much sense. I've forgotten what she said. My mother forbade me to ever speak to that woman again. I would have looked for her, asked her for explanations, but I decided it was best to let things be. Sometimes it's best to remain in ignorance."

Adelina nodded. Perhaps he was right. She wondered what the cleaning lady had tried to tell him. "Who was your cleaning lady?" she asked.

"A woman named Antonia," José Alberto said.

Adelina closed her eyes and thought about someone she'd known in the past whose name was Antonia. Her godmother.

"She used to look at me the way you look at me," José Alberto said.

"How?"

"As if you see in me someone you once knew."

• • •

The judicial guided them down the corridor to the clinic. Adelina felt her heart thumping hard against her chest. Why did she suddenly feel scared about bringing José Alberto along? Would Amá recognize him as the son she once lost? She wondered what José Alberto would say. She should have prepared him. Perhaps it would have been better to tell him herself, after all.

Amá was asleep when they got there. And asleep or not, the judicial said their visit would be for twenty minutes. José Alberto pulled up the only chair for Adelina to sit on. He remained standing. Adelina didn't know what to do. Part of her was relieved. She had wanted José Alberto to see his real mother at least once. And now he had. But she would have liked for Amá to see him also. She deserved to hold her son in her arms again, if only for a while.

They were silent. Adelina noticed that José Alberto wouldn't take his eyes off Amá. She wondered what he was thinking. She wanted to tell him that this was not how Amá had once been. She wanted to tell him that once Amá had been beautiful, and strong, before Don Elías took him away.

Amá opened her eyes, then blinked as if she couldn't believe what she saw. "Miguel? You've come back for me? You've come back?"

Amá held her arms out to him.

Adelina got to her feet and tried to get her mother to lean back on the pillow again.

"Amá, calm down, please. Lie down again."

Amá reached for José Alberto even more.

"Señora, it's okay, come, lie down." José Alberto gently grabbed Amá's hands, then helped her lie back down. Amá didn't let go of José Alberto's right hand.

"Miguel, you've come home. I knew you would come home. Where have you been?"

Adelina saw the tears sliding down Amá's wrinkled cheeks. Why hadn't she thought this would happen? Amá did not see in José Alberto the son she'd lost. She was seeing the husband she'd loved.

José Alberto put his left hand over Amá's hand and patted it. He seemed nearly as stunned as she. He turned to look at Adelina and asked, "What's your mother's name?"

"Lupe. Lupe García."

José Alberto turned back to Amá.

"We have a son, Miguel," Amá said to José Alberto. "I named him Miguel, after you. But they took him away from me. They took him away." She clutched José Alberto's hands and asked, "You'll bring him back, won't you, Miguel? You'll get our son back?"

José Alberto nodded. "Yes, Lupe. I'll find our son and bring him back so he can be with us, I promise."

Adelina was at a loss for words. All she could do was wonder what was going through José Alberto's mind. Amá leaned against him. He brought his hand up and slowly ran his fingers down Amá's hair.

"Okay, señorita, your twenty minutes are up." The judicial's voice startled them. "Please allow me to escort you back to the waiting area."

Adelina wanted to tell him to leave. Couldn't the officer

see how important this moment was? But she was too over-whelmed. So instead she turned to look at the officer and nodded. She walked over to the bed and bent down to kiss Amá's forehead.

"Amá, we must be going. We'll come visit you again in a few days, okay? But you have to promise me you're going to start eating—"

"But you can't leave. You can't," Amá said. She turned away from Adelina and looked at José Alberto. "Miguel, you can't leave again. You can't. Please not again."

Amá struggled to get out of the bed. She almost fell, but José Alberto rushed back to her side and steadied her. Amá clung to José Alberto's waist and refused to let him go. The judicial walked over to try to yank her away from José Alberto.

"I said visiting time is over!"

"Miguel, please don't leave me here. Please don't go!"

"I'll be back soon, Lupe, I promise," José Alberto said. The judicial motioned for him to step away from Amá. Adelina grabbed his arm and pulled him away. The judicial asked them to start walking to the door, and then called out for the doctor on duty.

"Please, Miguel, please!" Amá screamed.

José Alberto turned around and headed back to Amá's bed.

"Sir, you need to leave," the judicial said.

José Alberto didn't listen. He sat down on Amá's bed, pulled her into his arms, and whispered something in her ear. After a moment Amá stopped crying. She wiped her eyes dry and smiled.

When the doctor came, Amá leaned back on the pillow and let him inject her with a sedative that would make her sleep.

José Alberto sat on the bed, next to Amá, and held her hand as sleep began to claim her.

"You will keep your promise, right, Miguel? You'll keep your promise?" Amá said as she closed her eyes.

"Yes, Lupe. I will keep my promise."

Amá smiled, and was soon fast asleep.

"Señorita García," the doctor said to Adelina. "I believe it would be best if your mother was transferred to a psychiatric facility where her needs would be better met."

"But doctor—" Adelina began.

"Forgive me, señorita, but today I'll be talking to the supervisor about the transfer."

"Please, Doctor, just give her time. She'll pull out of this, I know she will."

"I'm sorry, señorita, but we've done everything we could do for her." The doctor motioned for the officer to walk Adelina and José Alberto out.

José Alberto grabbed Adelina's hand and squeezed it tight.

"Don't worry, we'll find a way to get her out of here," he said. "There has to be a way."

Adelina nodded. She grabbed his arm and followed the officer out to the corridor.

Adelina slept late the next day. She woke up with a pain in her chest, and her pillow was wet, as if she'd been crying in her dream.

And perhaps she had. She had dreamed of Sebastian.

She had dreamed about the night she told him to forget her, to never look for her again.

"I don't know what it is that's driving you away from me," he'd said. "But I hope one day you'll be free of it."

He had not looked for her again, just as she had asked him to.

Adelina pulled the blanket over her head, wishing it was still dark, wishing the telephone wasn't ringing in the living room, wishing dogs weren't barking outside. She didn't want to be awake. She wanted to sleep again, dream again, but this time she wanted to dream a good dream.

"Adelina, are you up yet? There's a call for you," Sandra said on the other side of the door.

Adelina yanked the blanket away in defeat. "Who is it?"

"It's from the prison. It's about your mother."

"I'll be right there," Adelina called out. She jumped out of bed, grabbed her robe, and rushed to the living room where Sandra was waiting for her. Adelina picked up the phone from the table and almost dropped it. She held on to it tighter as she put it against her ear.

"Bueno?"

"Is this Señorita Juana García, daughter of Guadalupe Ramírez de García?" a woman on the other end said.

"Yes, this is Juana," Adelina said. She glanced over at Sandra and noticed that she was biting her nails.

"Señorita, I'm sorry to deliver these sad news to you, but your mother passed away last night."

"What?" Adelina yelled into the phone receiver. Sandra came to stand next to her and leaned closer so that she could hear. "But she was fine yesterday. What happened?"

"Your mother suffered a heart attack late last night. The doctor and nurses tried to save her, but they couldn't get her back. She was too weak."

"But—"

"I'm sorry, Señorita García. You must come claim your mother's body as soon as possible. The doctors will answer any questions you might have. When will you be arriving?"

Adelina looked at Sandra from the corner of her eye. She was shaking her head in disbelief. "I will come today."

"Very well. And again, I'm sorry."

When the line went dead Sandra took the phone from Adelina. Adelina slowly made her way to the couch and let herself sink into it.

"I don't understand," Sandra said. "How could this happen?"

Adelina didn't know what to say. Her mother was dead.

"She made this happen," Sandra said. "Lupe made herself die."

"I wanted her to die in peace," Adelina said. "I don't know if she did."

Sandra came to sit beside Adelina and put her arms around her. "I'm sure she did, Adelina, I'm sure she did. You brought her husband and her son to her. You brought her daughter back. She must have been happy."

Adelina buried her face in her hands. She let Sandra pull her against her bosom, then closed her eyes tight. She let the tears flow. She had cried when she was asleep, and now she was crying when she was awake. And both times hurt as much.

They sat in silence for a while. Sandra stroked Adelina's hair. It had been so long since someone had touched her in a motherly way. She leaned against the older woman.

They would have sat there longer if someone hadn't knocked on the door. It was José Alberto. "May I please speak to Juana?"

Adelina sat up on the couch and turned to the door. She slowly rose to her feet but didn't even attempt to take a step forward. She stayed rooted to the floor.

"I'm sorry to bother you," José Alberto said, "but I need to speak with you."

Adelina noticed the paleness of his face and his slightly red eyes, as if he'd been crying. What was the matter?

"You're not bothering me," Adelina said. "Come, have a seat."

Sandra excused herself and left for the kitchen to get drinks. José Alberto put down the backpack he carried over one shoulder and sat down next to Adelina.

When he turned to her, and Adelina looked into his tear-shaped eyes, she couldn't hold herself back and began to cry once again.

Their mother was dead and he wouldn't ever know this.

"Hey, what's wrong? Tell me, what's the matter?" José Alberto took Adelina's hands into his. She gripped them tight, afraid to let him go.

"She's dead," she said.

"Who?"

"My mother."

José Alberto shook his head in disbelief. "But how? When?"

"Last night. She had a heart attack."

José Alberto leaned back against the couch and shook his head once again. "I can't believe it. I'm just afraid to think that maybe it was my fault."

"Why would it be your fault?" Adelina asked as she rubbed her eyes dry.

"Maybe she was shocked. Maybe it was too much for her, to let her think I was her husband. I shouldn't have let her think that."

"No, don't say that. She needed it. She needed to think that my father had come back to her. I think that is what she was waiting for, so that she could die in peace."

José Alberto closed his eyes. Adelina wondered what he was thinking.

"When will you go claim the body?" he asked after a brief moment.

"I'm leaving in an hour, after I get my things ready."

José Alberto looked at Adelina and said, "I'm coming with you."

Adelina declined to see her mother's body before it was cremated. She didn't want the image of her dead mother to blur all the memories she held in her mind, memories of her mother when she was young. Before the flood. Before Anita drowned. Before Don Elías came into their lives.

José Alberto did go see Amá. Adelina wondered why. It was as if he knew who Amá was to him. Anyone else wouldn't have even bothered to accompany her all the way to Chilpancingo. Adelina had to admit that Doña Matilde had instilled in him all the values Amá wanted her son to have.

Amá's ashes were put inside a small tin box. José Alberto carried it in his hand while Adelina held the wooden box that contained her father's ashes.

They spent the night at a small hotel in the center of downtown. Adelina couldn't sleep. She wondered if José Alberto, who had gotten a room across from hers, was sleeping.

Her little brother.

What wouldn't she give to call him hermano at least once. What wouldn't she give to be able to hold him, to hear him call her sister. She should have put her pride and anger aside, and she should have rocked him, sang to him, held him tight. But how was she to know Don Elías would come and take him away?

There was a tap on the door.

"Who is it?" Adelina said into the darkness. She reached over to the nightstand and turned on the lamp.

"It's José Alberto."

Adelina peeled back the covers and stood up to open the door.

"Did I wake you?" José Alberto asked.

Adelina shook her head. She motioned for him to come in and then closed the door.

"I can't sleep," she said.

José Alberto nodded. "Neither can I."

They sat down on the bed. José Alberto looked down at his hands, as if he was thinking about what to say.

"I know who you are," he finally said.

Adelina gripped the corner of the bed comforter. "What do you mean?"

José Alberto turned to look at her and said, "I know you're my sister. I know the ashes inside that tin box belong to my real mother, and I know the husband she had been waiting for was my father. That's what I mean."

She got up and picked up her white rosary from the night-stand and began to finger the beads. "Who told you?"

"Antonia."

"You went to look for her?"

"Yes, I did."

Adelina went to stand by the window. Through the crack between the curtains she could see the moon peeking through the bare branches of a tree. "Why did you do that?"

"Because I wanted to know the truth. Because every time I look at you I know there's something you want to tell me, yet you can't bring yourself to do it." José Alberto got up and came to stand beside her. "I see the way my— Doña Matilde acts around you, and the way you are with her. You two know each other. When you say things to one another there are so many words that go unsaid, and yet you seem to hear them anyway. They are silent words only you two comprehend. And there's your mother."

"What about her?"

"She mistook me for her husband and called me Miguel. Only one person had ever called me that by mistake."

"Who?"

"Antonia. I was ten years old, but I still remember it. The name just escaped her lips, and when I asked her about it she told me it was because I reminded her of her compadre Miguel, whom she hadn't seen in a long time."

"So what did she tell you when you went to see her?" Adelina nervously ran her fingers over each bead of the rosary, mumbling an Our Father under her breath.

"She told me what she could remember about o-our mother, about you, about our father. She told me what Don Elías had done to our mother."

Adelina walked back to the bed and sat down.

"Did she tell you about Anita?" she asked, feeling the familiar guilt choke her up inside.

He nodded.

"There was one child she lost because of me," she said.

"Juana," José Alberto came to stand in front of her and knelt down on one knee. He took her hand in his and looked at her. "She got her son back because of you, don't forget that."

"I'm sorry you had to find out that way," she said.

"You thought it was better I didn't know?"

Adelina nodded.

"You are my sister," José Alberto said.

Adelina felt her tears quickly rush to her eyes. "Yes, I am. And you're my little brother," she said. "Mi hermanito. And I have always loved you."

José Alberto put his head on her lap. She felt his body give a slight tremor before they both began to weep.

They didn't return to the town. Instead, Adelina decided to travel to Acapulco, only an hour or so away.

"Why do you want to go there?" José Alberto asked.

"To take my mother to see the ocean."

Amá had never seen the ocean in person, but at least in death she would get to see it. She would get to feel the wind ruffle her hair. She would get to feel the cool water drip down her legs. She would get to taste the water's saltiness on her lips. This was the last thing Adelina would do for her mother.

They waited until the sun hung a few inches above the horizon. They both stood on a rock, directly above the water. Adelina watched the waves splash against the rocks. The setting sun cast a golden reddish glow on the water. She looked directly at the sun. At this time, it had already lost its bright glare, and it didn't hurt her eyes to look at it.

"Are you ready?" José Alberto asked.

Adelina nodded.

They held out their parents' ashes. Adelina carried the wooden box and José Alberto the tin box. They held them out in front of them and chanted an Our Father and a Hail Mary. Then they both began to say their own distinct prayers, but not prayers they had learned as children in their catechism classes, but prayers they now made up, telling their parents everything they felt in their hearts.

Then, when they finished, Adelina and José Alberto stepped forward to the very edge of the rock. They turned the boxes upside down and let their parents' ashes float down below, settling over the water.

Adelina took her white rosary from her pocket, held it out in front of her, and then let it fall from her hand, down into the foamy water. She turned to look at José Alberto and nodded. He walked back to the backpack he had left on the ground and picked it up. He took something out that was wrapped in newspaper.

"I have something for you," he said as he slowly began unwrapping the bundle he held in his hand. When he held it up Adelina gasped.

She looked at the perfectly round circle made of porcelain, adorned with purple lilacs and pink butterflies.

It was a plate. It was the last plate left of her mother's plate set. The plate Amá hadn't thrown against the rock the day she gave herself to Don Elías. Adelina had forgotten all about it.

"Where did you get that?" she asked.

"Antonia gave it to me."

"But where did she get it?"

"Mamá gave it to her one day. She told her what she'd done with the rest of the plates, and she wanted to save at least one for you. She didn't trust herself with it, that's why she gave it to Antonia to keep."

"I'm surprised Antonia didn't throw it away. She didn't want to talk to Amá once she learned Amá was pregnant with who she thought was Don Elías's child."

"She said she couldn't bring herself to do it. So she saved it, as she had promised." José Alberto handed the plate to Adelina. She reached out for it and held it in her hands. The plate set had been meant for her to use one day when she got married.

"It gave me and your father good luck, Juana. We've had a good marriage," Amá had often told her when she talked about the set of plates.

"It's yours, Juana," José Alberto said. "It's your inheritance."

Adelina took a breath of the ocean's scent. The smell reminded her of Sebastian.

He had said he would wait for her.

Juana turned to look at the ghostly moon that was now preparing to begin a new journey across the sky. She breathed in the ocean air and felt the spray on her legs as the waves crashed on the rocks below.

acknowledgments

I want to thank everyone who directly or indirectly helped me make this novel a reality.

I especially thank the Emerging Voices Rosenthal Fellowship program for helping me grow as a writer. Thank you, Teena Apeles, for making my experience in the program a most memorable one.

A big thank-you goes to my former mentor, writer María Amparo Escandón, for all the good advice and encouragement.

Jenoyne Adams, my wonderful agent, for believing in this novel even before it was finished.

Ibarionex Perello, for reading the first drafts and making valued suggestions.

A most sincere thank-you to my teacher, friend, mentor Diana Savas for realizing, even before I did, that I was a writer.

My creative writing teachers, especially Micah Perks, for guiding me down the right path.

To everyone at Atria Books, for helping me make this book the best that it could be.

And finally to Cory, for always listening when I wanted to talk about the novel, for questioning, encouraging, and above all, for always being there when I needed you.

about the author

Reyna Grande was born in Guerrero, Mexico, in 1975. When she was five years old, her father and mother immigrated to the United States and left her and her siblings in care of her grandmother. She entered the United States as an illegal immigrant in 1985. She graduated from the University of California, Santa Cruz, in 1999, with a B.A. in creative writing and film & video. She was a PEN USA West Emerging Voices Fellow in 2003. She lives in Los Angeles.

For more information about Reyna Grande,
visit www.reynagrande.com.